BLACK STAR'S CAMPAIGN

BLACK STAR'S CAMPAIGN

Johnston McCulley

WILDSIDE PRESS

Published by Wildside Press, LLC
www.wildsidebooks.com

CHAPTER I

NEWS FOR THE SHERIFF

Sheriff Kowen looked up from his desk in amazement as the stenographer ushered in the woman. The name on her card had told him nothing, and he had expected to be confronted by some middle-aged, washed-out, tired wife and mother who would make a request to visit the jail and talk with an erring relative.

What he did see when he raised his eyes and cleared his throat preparatory to indulging in his professional attitude, was a handsomely gowned, beautiful woman of perhaps thirty years, a woman who appeared to be exceedingly cultured and refined.

Sheriff Kowen got out of his chair quickly, and placed one at the end of the desk for his visitor. Then he seated himself again, and looked across to her.

She appeared to be nervous, almost distraught, on the verge of tears.

"My dear Miss Blanchard," Sheriff Kowen said, glancing at the card the stenographer had handed to him, and for once forgetting his usual gruff manner, "is there any way in which I may be of service to you?"

"I scarcely know how to approach the subject," she replied. The sheriff noticed that her voice was all that he had expected it would be—a voice that was modulated to the correct society pitch. "Such a thing as—as this is—well, I am not used to it."

"Just take your time, and tell me in your own way," said the sheriff. "You have—er—some sort of a complaint to make?"

"Yes, that is it. In the first place, we do not reside in this city regularly. We have a suite at a private hotel—my mother, my brother and myself. It is about my brother that I wish to see you."

"He is—er—in trouble?"

"Not exactly that, but—please tell me, first, Mr. Kowen, it is against the law to operate a gambling house, is it not?"

"It most certainly is!" Kowen exclaimed. "When I was first elected, I fought gambling houses—got quite a reputation for working along that line. I fought the cheap ones, and I fought the pretentious dress-suit establishments—cleaned them out!"

"Pardon me, Mr. Kowen, but one remains—else it is a new one that has opened recently."

"What's that?" the sheriff cried, sitting up straighter in his chair. "If there is a gambling house running in my section of the country, it'll not run long!"

"I—I feel almost like a spy," Miss Blanchard said. "I hate to be an informer—"

"That is your duty in such a case, my dear young lady."

"I feel it so, under the circumstances," she said. "I do not want to cause my brother trouble—but I have talked it over with mother, and we decided that I should come and tell you the whole thing."

"I shall be glad to listen, Miss Blanchard."

"My brother is twenty-one, just a boy, you might say. When we came to the city, he happened to make the acquaintance of some other young men who belonged to a very fast set. He began remaining away from home until the early morning hours, and drinking too much, and all that."

"I understand, my dear young lady. Nine young men out of ten sow their wild oats."

"And he began spending more money than he could afford to spend. Mother and I began to fear he would dissipate his share of my father's estate, for he controls it since he has come of age. We wondered where the money was going—and finally we found out."

"Gambling joint?"

"Yes, sir. A gambling den in a large house in the most exclusive section of the city."

"Those are the places I like to smash!" Sheriff Kowen told her.

"I can give you the address, Mr. Kowen. I understand that a man cannot get into the place unless he is properly introduced."

"Naturally, they would be very careful," the sheriff said.

"It is what you called a dress-suit sort of place. Perhaps I am doing wrong telling you this—"

"Not at all. It is your duty," the sheriff assured her. "Nobody ever will know where I got my information."

"I'd like to have the place closed up," Miss Blanchard continued, "so that my brother and other young men will not be robbed of their money and ruined. I suppose you would have to make a raid—I believe that is the term? I'd hate to cause my brother trouble, but a little scare might—"

"I understand, Miss Blanchard. It is probable that he would be caught in a raid, placed under arrest for frequenting a gambling resort, and brought to jail. He would immediately put up bail for his appearance in court. He would give an assumed name, and not show up in the morning, forfeiting his bail. So there would be little publicity, but he would get a scare."

"Oh, thank you! If it could be done that way—"

"It can, my dear Miss Blanchard. We are determined to exterminate gambling houses. The court is in accord with me in this matter. Since you give me the information, you may be sure I'll protect your brother's interests to a certain extent. We'll frighten him a bit, but you need have no fear he will serve a term in jail, or anything like that."

"I understand," said Miss Blanchard.

"Simply give me the address—and then forget that you have seen and spoken to me. I'll do the rest. You must be very careful, of course, not to let your brother suspect that you have been here. He would inform his friends, and our raid would fail. Every time a raid fails, it hurts us. A certain part of the public, antagonistic politicians and newspapers, you see—"

"I understand, Mr. Kowen. Here is the address—I have written it on a card."

She placed the card before him on the desk. Sheriff Kowen glanced at it.

"Ah!" he exclaimed. "So! I should say it was in the most exclusive section of the city. This is very valuable information, Miss Blanchard, if our investigation bears out your statements. I cannot thank you enough. There will be more to this than a gambling-house raid; the owners of the property must give the court a little explanation, I fear."

"You are sure that I did not do wrong coming here like this?"

"I am sure that you did quite right, my dear young lady. You perhaps have aided us in rounding up sharpers who fleece young men of their fortunes, and perhaps you have saved your brother. He is at the stage, I take it, where a little scare will do him a lot of good. You have done quite right!"

"Then I must hurry away," she said, rising. "And I shall do as you said—forget that I have been here. My brother—"

"I'll watch out for him, Miss Blanchard—a little scare and nothing more! It is the proprietor of the place and his partners we are after, more than the victims."

Sheriff Kowen went as far as the corridor with Miss Blanchard, and then hurried back to his private office and began pushing buttons. He called before him certain of his deputies, gave them the information he had acquired, and certain orders, and sent them away. Then he touched match to cigar, leaned back in his chair, blew a cloud of fragrant smoke toward the ceiling, and chuckled softly. Sheriff Kowen had not had a chance to raid a gambling house of any importance for more than a year; and raiding a gambling house was his pet sport. He promised himself that this raid should be sensational in the extreme. Gambling houses were not going to flourish while Kowen was holding office as sheriff.

As for Miss Blanchard, she drove in a taxicab to an exclusive private hotel, ascended in the elevator to the eighth floor, and entered a suite there.

A woman of forty was sitting before a window looking down at the busy street. She was talking to a man of about the same age, a man who appeared to be a prosperous merchant, or something of the sort, and who looked up quickly when Miss Blanchard entered.

"Well, Mamie, how about it?" he growled.

"It was easy!" Miss Mamie Blanchard replied. "He fell for it so hard that I could almost see him bounce. He swallowed the bait, hook, sinker and line. We've played the game just right—that man would rather raid a gambling joint than eat!"

"Think he'll get busy right away?" the man asked.

"Busy? The instant he left me he ran back to his desk. I think that we can look for action tonight."

"Well, we'll give him a chance. He'll want to make sure of the evidence first, of course, and we'll see that he gathers plenty of that without too much trouble. All the other details have been arranged. I'll issue orders this afternoon, and have everything in readiness. We can't go wrong on this."

"And afterward?" the girl asked.

"You'll get your reward, all right. If this man's town isn't crazy within forty-eight hours, it'll be something peculiar. You know your part, I suppose?"

"Certainly."

"Get ready, then. I'll go, now, and get word to all the boys. I'm glad that the long wait is over, that we are ready to strike!"

CHAPTER II

A SHOCK FOR THE CITY

The deputies sent forth by Sheriff Kowen did their work well, and without experiencing much difficulty. Their investigations were concluded before nightfall, and the sheriff rubbed his hands together in glee when he received their reports.

At eleven o'clock that night, he sat at his desk and answered telephone calls. At a certain place near the gambling house his men had gathered. Kowen knew from experience that it did not do to have them meet at his office or the county jail. There always was somebody watching, and any unusual activity would cause a warning to be flashed to every resort that had reason to expect a raid.

"It's all right, boss," one of his deputies telephoned. "We've been on the watch since eight o'clock. There are about thirty men in the place now, and more coming all the time. They're pretty bold about it—feel safe, I reckon."

"That's because they've been getting away with it for a few months," the sheriff replied. "We'll make 'em sick before morning."

He finished smoking his cigar; then left the office and walked down the street to the corner, as he always did at that hour of the night. That was to make things appear natural, if anybody happened to be watching. He waited for a surface car, got aboard, and started home. At a certain corner, he alighted in order to transfer to another line.

But Sheriff Kowen did not use his transfer tonight. He made sure that nobody was watching him, and then darted down a side street. He pulled his hat over his eyes, bent his shoulders forward, and walked rapidly down the broad avenue toward the exclusive residential section of the city.

He had a mile to walk. He covered three fourths of it at a good pace, and then slowed down and became more alert. He passed another man on a corner.

"All right, boss," the man whispered.

"All right!" Sheriff Kowen answered.

Kowen went on up the street. He stopped in a dark spot beneath an overhanging tree, and looked at a house in the middle of the block. He knew the property; it belonged to an old estate, and was handled by a well-known real estate firm. For years it had been without a tenant. The investigation made by the deputies during the afternoon had resulted in the information that it had been repaired and leased some three months before to strangers in the city, but people who had exhibited good references.

It was some distance away from the other residences, and the lot was bordered by a high hedge, except in front. It was an ideal location for a fashionable gambling resort.

As Kowen watched, he saw a young man saunter down the street, hesitate a moment, then enter the gate and hurry toward the house.

"Another victim!" Kowen told himself.

Now one of his deputies approached him, keeping in the shadows as much as possible.

"Well?" Kowen snapped.

"Almost forty men in there, boss," the deputy reported.

"All our crowd ready?"

"Yes."

"What time is it?"

"Quarter after twelve. I looked at my watch as I walked under the light at the corner."

"Let's get in action then," Kowen said. "I don't want any slips, now. I want to gather in the whole lot. Got the autos ready?"

"They're ready, boss, waiting down the street a couple of

blocks."

"Signal them up, and we'll begin."

The deputy hurried away. Sheriff Kowen crossed the street, turned in through the gate, and blew a whistle.

On every side, deputies rushed toward the house, surrounding it immediately. Kowen ran up the steps and knocked at the door. An aperture was opened, a face peered out, there was an exclamation, and the aperture was closed again.

"Into it!" Kowen cried.

Deputies ran forward with axes and attacked the heavy door. The door at the rear was attacked in the same manner. Some of the men guarded the entrance to the basement, others watched the windows closely.

The front door crashed down, and the officers poured into the house. From the second floor came a chorus of cries and shrieks. The lights had been extinguished, and electric torches flashed.

"Watch those stairs!" Kowen cried. "Some of you clean out the basement—I want the entire crowd! I'll go above!"

They made their way to the head of the stairs, smashed through another door, flashed their torches, found the light switch and turned it. The big room was bathed in light.

Sheriff Kowen smiled grimly as he surveyed the scene. He saw faro and roulette layouts, poker tables, almost every gambling device known. Some two score of men in evening dress were crouching against the walls. A glance was enough to tell the sheriff the customers and the dealers. He slapped his hands together.

"Round 'em up!" he ordered.

His deputies sprang to obey. One by one, the men in the room were manacled, despite their protests. When Sheriff Kowen raided a gambling house, he did not do things by halves.

A crowd had collected in the street by now. The automobiles Kowen had ordered were before the house, ready to receive their loads of prisoners. Kowen received reports from deputies who had searched the place from cellar to garret. He detailed men to guard the house and the gambling apparatus it contained, and then the parade began.

The parade was always a big moment with Kowen. He stood at the curb and watched the prisoners pass him and go to the automobiles. He enjoyed the looks of wrath, of fear in the faces of these callow youths. Some of them he knew, but a very few. For the most part, the prisoners seemed to be strangers to him, but that did not bother Kowen. The city was a large one; a new crop of victims appeared every week, the sheriff knew.

The prisoners were driven to the county jail and taken into the office. Kowen informed them as to the charges, and announced that bail would be one hundred dollars in each case, except that of the proprietor of the place. The jailer and bookkeeper got ready.

It was then that Sheriff Kowen got his first surprise. With the exception of the proprietor, none of his prisoners would furnish bail. The arrest was an outrage, they declared. They had been informed that the ordinance against gambling was unconstitutional. They were going to jail, going to fight the case, and then sue for damages. They'd show Sheriff Kowen and his men that citizens had rights that should be respected.

"Are you a bunch of lunatics?" Kowen cried. "Don't you worry about that gambling law—we've convicted many a man on it, men who had coin to fight their cases, too. And let me tell you men something—if you go into cells, your right names go down on the blotter. They'll go into the newspapers, too; and the people of this city will know just who the men are who smash laws and waste money!"

"We're not worrying any about that stuff!" one of the prisoners told him.

"Then you'll be searched and slammed into cells, believe me! And you'll be treated like ordinary prisoners. I have a faint idea that you'll be dead willing to put up bail by noon. These cells of mine are not comfortable suites. And you'll miss your baths and grapefruit in the morning, and your thin toast! Well?"

None made reply. Kowen glanced around the room at them, and then an angry flush came into his face. He had half a dozen deputies there, and the night jailer and the bookkeeper. He had let the other deputies go, thinking this would be like other raids, that the prisoners would put up bail immediately or telephone for it, and hurry to their homes.

"Line up against that wall!" he commanded. "If you are so eager to go to jail, we can accommodate you, all right. The jailer will search you."

The jailer appeared before the first man, who started taking things from his pockets. Sheriff Kowen turned his back and started for his private office in disgust. Newspapermen were waiting there for him, and the sheriff did not dislike publicity.

Then something strange happened!

With the exceptions of the few men known to the sheriff, every prisoner drew something from his pocket. Something seemed to crash against the floor. There was a series of sharp explosions, and the office and rooms adjoining were filled with clouds of white, pungent smoke.

The jailer opened his mouth to shout a warning, and toppled over on the floor without having spoken. Here and there the deputies were dropping, none of them having time to get out a revolver and fire a shot. Sheriff Kowen rushed in from his private office to have a cloud of the pungent vapor strike him full in the face. The newspaper reporters suffered a like fate.

The prisoners were holding tiny sponges to their nostrils, and now they sprang into action. Some rushed to the street door and locked and barred it. Others drew the shades at the windows. One searched the jailer and got his keys, and hurried toward the door leading into the corridor.

This door was opened. Four of the prisoners rushed down

the aisle and came to a certain cell. Inside it a man was sitting on a bunk.

"Good work!" he exclaimed.

The door of the cell was unlocked, and the man stepped out. He led the way back to the office, glanced around it quickly.

"Everything done?" he asked.

"Everything done, sir," one of the men replied.

"Let's go, then!"

The street door was unlocked. Around the corner came half a dozen automobiles. They were filled, and darted away, scattering as they came to the first street corner.

* * * *

Sheriff Kowen groaned and opened his eyes. One of his deputies was just regaining consciousness. The sheriff tried to get to his feet.

"What—what—" he began.

"They're all gone—jail door's open," the deputy gasped.

"It—I know! Vapor bombs!" Kowen cried. "More Black Star work! Quick—look—"

Kowen had managed to get to his feet now, and was rushing into the corridor of the jail. More deputies were regaining consciousness. The sheriff pushed past them and ran down the corridor. They heard him cry out.

"Gone—gone!" he shrieked. "The Black Star has escaped! It was all a trick—that woman, the gambling joint—a trick to get all those men in here so they could do their work—"

"Here's a note in the cell!" a deputy cried.

The sheriff took it and ran back to the office. One of the deputies already was telephoning police headquarters and relating the story. The Black Star had been rescued! The supercriminal who had been tried and convicted, who was to start for the State prison on the following day, had made his escape!

On the brow of each unconscious man left behind by the

band there had been pasted a tiny black star—the criminal's mark. There was a row of them on the blotter-sheet. They were on the walls, on the casements.

The reporters rushed for telephones. Here was news that would startle the city in the morning. Was the town in for another reign of crime? Would the notorious Black Star merely make good his escape, or did he have plans perfected? Was his band reorganized? Would he take vengeance for his arrest and incarceration?

The note found in the cell supplied the answer. Sheriff Kowen read it quickly:

> To Whom It May Concern:
> Did you think for an instant that the Black Star would go to prison to serve twenty years? It was a very clever rescue, was it not? And for the months I have been held in jail, for the strain and worry of my trial, I am going to make the city pay. My organization is more perfect than before. My plans have been well made. The city shall pay—pay—pay! And tell that fool of a Roger Verbeck, who was instrumental in catching me before, that he will be helpless this time. I defy him even to find the location of my headquarters.

* * * *

All the telephones were busy now. The pungent odor that had come from the vapor bombs had blown out of the room. Word was being flashed over the city that the Black Star had been rescued by his band, and that he had promised a wave of crime to pay for his incarceration.

Nobody doubted that such would be the case. The city knew well that the Black Star always made good his boasts. Nobody doubted that his organization was greater than it had been before, and that clever plans had been made.

The Black Star, they had reason to suppose, would not wait very long before striking, for that was not his nature. The city faced the great question:

Where would the Black Star strike first?

CHAPTER III

THE NEW HEADQUARTERS

Roger Verbeck was the last of his family, a man who moved in the best social circles, who had wealth and good looks and friends, and an athletic body.

It had been Roger Verbeck who had put the Black Star behind prison bars. When the supercriminal first began his work in the city, the police seemed to be unable to do anything against him. Verbeck had made a boast at a reception one night that he could capture the Black Star himself. That boast had led to many adventures.

One of the Black Star's band happened to overhear the boast, for the men and women working for the Black Star were to be found in all walks of life, and there was nothing strange in the fact that one of them happened to be a guest at an exclusive social affair. At one stage of the game even Verbeck himself had been suspected of being a lieutenant of the master criminal.

The Black Star had challenged Verbeck to make good his boast, and there had ensued a duel of wits. Whereas the master rogue had an organization at his command, Verbeck had nobody except Muggs.

Muggs was a peculiar individual. Years before, Muggs had stood on a bridge over the Seine, in Paris, ready to fling himself into the water and end an existence that, in a fit of despondency, he had decided was not worth carrying out to its logical conclusion.

Roger Verbeck had grasped him by the arm in time to save him, and had convinced Muggs that life was worth the living. So Muggs became attached to Roger Verbeck. He was known as Verbeck's valet, but he was a comrade-in-arms in reality.

He shared Verbeck's adventures, and often turned failure into success. He was ready to fight for Verbeck at any moment.

Muggs had worked with Verbeck against the Black Star, and when the master criminal finally was captured and incarcerated, Muggs had turned valet again. But Muggs was a man who demanded action, and time hung heavy on his hands. For Roger Verbeck was thinking of getting married, and he had small time for adventuring.

Muggs was a small man, but one of great strength. There was nothing handsome about him. Some called him repulsive, but not in Roger Verbeck's hearing.

Muggs had been a criminal and knew the ways of criminals. He had been of great value to Verbeck on numerous occasions, and once had saved his life. Between them they possessed nearly all human qualifications, and they made an excellent team.

On the night of the rescue of the Black Star, Roger Verbeck had called upon his fiancée. He returned to his rooms shortly after the hour of twelve, and immediately went to bed, Muggs retiring a few minutes later. There was to be a golf tournament the following day, and Verbeck was a contestant.

Both men were asleep almost immediately. Most of the tenants in the big apartment house had retired. In the office on the ground floor a sleepy clerk was attempting to keep his eyes open and read a magazine. The night telephone operator had gone to a restaurant a couple of blocks away for a midnight cup of coffee, and the sleepy clerk was watching the switchboard.

There entered a gentleman from the street—a man whose face was muffled in his coat collar. He was well-dressed, very much the gentleman, and the clerk got up and hurried to the desk. Somebody with an important business message for one of the tenants, the clerk supposed.

"Something I can do for you, sir?" the clerk asked.

"Yes—go to sleep!" came the reply.

The visitor drew a vapor gun and discharged it in the clerk's face. The latter gasped, and sank to the floor. The one who had used the gun stepped to the door and gave a signal. Three more men sprang from a closed car standing at the curb, and hurried into the lobby of the house.

"Telephone operator be back in a few minutes," the first man said. "One of you remain here and get him. Answer any calls on the switchboard, so things will look natural."

One remained; the other three ran quickly up the stairs, ignoring the elevator, which was in the basement, with a sleepy operator hoping that nobody would call him.

The three made their way to the floor where Roger Verbeck had his suite. They listened outside Verbeck's door; then one of them inserted a skeleton key, pushed out the key on the inside, turned the lock and opened the door half a dozen inches.

Again they listened, then opened the door wider and slipped inside. It was evident that they were well acquainted with the place. While one of them remained in the big living room, another went to the door of Verbeck's bedchamber, and a third to the door of the room used by Muggs.

There came a sharp hiss. The doors were opened. Figures darted across rooms. Two vapor guns were discharged, and Roger Verbeck and Muggs were instantly rendered unconscious as they slept.

"Easy work!" one of the men commented. "Get busy, now!"

Muggs was gagged and bound and lashed to the bed. Roger Verbeck was dressed quickly by two of the men, while the third remained in the living room, listening. When Verbeck had been made ready, the man in the living room slipped into the hall, saw that nobody was there and that the elevator was still in the basement. He returned and gave a signal, and the other two picked up Verbeck and carried him into the hall.

They went down the stairs, flight by flight, meeting nobody, and finally came to the office again, where the fourth man was waiting. The telephone operator had returned and had been rendered unconscious by means of a vapor gun.

They carried Verbeck to the automobile, put him in it, got in themselves, and the machine darted away. Verbeck groaned, and once more a vapor gun was discharged in his face. He relaxed.

"That'll do him until we get to headquarters," one of the men said. "We don't want him sick, and that stuff is pretty strong. What do you suppose the boss is going to do with him?"

"It is an excellent plan not to go supposing what the boss is going to do with anybody," another growled. "I was in the other gang, and I happen to know that it's a good thing to let the boss attend to his own affairs."

"Well, I didn't mean anything," snarled the other.

The automobile traveled across the city, and after a time reached a large house that sat far back on a quiet lane. Here the car left the main thoroughfare, turned into the lane, and presently stopped before the veranda of the house. Roger Verbeck was carried inside. The automobile was driven around to the rear, and all its lights extinguished immediately.

When Verbeck regained consciousness he was bewildered. He was in a room that was brilliantly lighted. He was stretched upon a couch, fully dressed. He could not comprehend it at all.

He sat up and looked around the room. It was lavishly furnished, and in excellent taste. In the middle of the room was a long table, and there were a score of heavy chairs scattered about. There were two doors, one at either end of the room, but there did not seem to be any windows. Here and there tapestries hung on the walls.

He heard a bell tinkle, and one of the doors opened. There entered two men, both wearing long black robes, and black masks.

Verbeck knew, then. He had seen the costume of the members of the Black Star's band often before. He had even worn one once, while gathering evidence for use against the master criminal.

So he had been abducted by the Black Star's men, and he had supposed that they were so scattered that they could make no move. Was he to be held as hostage, or something like that? Verbeck knew that the Black Star was to be taken to prison within twenty-four hours. Were these men going to avenge themselves upon him because he had been instrumental in sending their leader to prison?

"Well?" Verbeck growled.

Neither man answered him, but he really had not expected that. The members of the Black Star's band did not talk much. One of the men went to the side of the room, and threw back one of the tapestries, revealing a small blackboard.

Why, this was exactly like the old headquarters of the Black Star, for they had conversed there by means of blackboards! Could it be possible that the band had gathered again, and were going to continue their nefarious work without their leader, the master mind that had guided and controlled them before?

Verbeck watched as the man wrote:

Mr. Verbeck will remain quietly on the couch for the time being. If he does not, he shall be made unconscious again.

"What is the idea?" Verbeck asked.

"One is coming who wishes to hold a conversation with you," the man wrote on the blackboard.

"How long shall I have to wait?" Verbeck demanded.

"Until he comes!" the other wrote, and then dropped the tapestry and went to stand beside his companion before the door.

Verbeck sat down on the couch again and regarded them. He felt in his pocket, found cigarettes and matches, and started smoking. His brain was not entirely clear yet.

He wondered what the man had meant. Who was the person for whom he was waiting? Of course, it couldn't be the Black

Star, Verbeck told himself. The Black Star was to go to prison the following day, to begin serving his sentence of twenty years. He had lost his last appeal. He had been a broken man, evidently, for the past two or three months had acted like one who had given up all hope of escape.

Verbeck smoked the cigarette and lighted another. Again a bell tinkled in the distance. Again the door was opened. Roger Verbeck gasped.

The robed and masked figure that entered was larger than the other men; and on the front of the hood that enveloped his head was a big, flaming black star of jet.

The Black Star!

Then Verbeck chuckled. He saw it now, of course. The band had elected another leader, and he had assumed the garb of the Black Star. Probably they expected to punish Roger Verbeck for what he had done.

The man who wore the star advanced to the middle of the room. One hand came from beneath his robe, and Verbeck saw that he held a vapor gun in it. He made a motion, and the other two men left the room and closed the door.

"So we have a new Black Star, have we?" Verbeck said.

The man before him laughed, then took off his mask and tossed it aside.

"Not a new one! The same one!" he said.

Verbeck gave a cry and sprang from the couch. There could be no mistake. The notorious master rogue stood before him. Verbeck knew his face well enough.

"But—" he began.

"My friends rescued me during the night," the Black Star said. "It was a very pretty little plot, indeed. I may as well let you know that I am heading my organization again. My people have been collected by a lieutenant of mine who never ceased working while I was in your county jail. My band is stronger than it was before, and we are going to make the city pay."

"Well, what about me?" Verbeck asked.

"I have had you brought here to show you in what contempt I hold you," the master criminal said. "You caught me before, but you'll not catch me again! Here is my new headquarters—take a good look. I suppose you'll be on my trail again?"

"And I'll catch you again!" Verbeck cried.

"It will be a pleasure to have you try, Mr. Verbeck. It adds spice to the game to have a good foe—and I'll admit that you are a good foe. It will be entertaining to outwit you continually, to make you the laughingstock of the city."

"You tried that once before, and I had the last laugh!"

"Pardon me! It is not time for the last laugh yet—but when the time does come, I shall have it!"

"Well, what are you going to do with me?" Verbeck demanded.

"My dear Mr. Verbeck! Did you imagine you were to be treated with violence? You know that I abhor violence of all kinds. I merely had you brought here so that we could have this little conversation. I shall send a letter to the newspapers telling them how I had you here and let you see my new headquarters. That will give the city its first laugh at you."

"If I get the chance, I'll catch you!" Verbeck declared.

"I intend you shall have the chance, my dear Mr. Verbeck. I shall render you unconscious again, and have you taken to a certain place in the city and left there. When you regain consciousness, start on my trail, if you can find it. You were unconscious when you came here, and will be when you depart. You understand? And I don't mind telling you, Roger Verbeck, that anything done by me and my band before my arrest was insignificant compared to what we intend doing now. I shall strike within twenty-four hours, Mr. Verbeck. You need not trouble to warn the city. I already have sent letters to the papers telling them of my intention."

"And you can't get away with it!" Verbeck exclaimed. "I'll

hunt you down—"

"That is your privilege, Mr. Verbeck," the Black Star interrupted. "I flatter myself that I am a sportsman. I have you in my power at the present moment, and could keep you where you could cause me no trouble or annoyance. But I'd rather have you free to use your wits against mine. As I remarked before, it will add spice to the game. Heaven knows that the police couldn't even make it interesting for me!"

"So you are going to stagger the city, are you?" Verbeck asked.

"I am, Mr. Verbeck. We are going to loot the city more thoroughly than we did before. We have perfected certain plans, and shall strike soon."

"Going to play your old game—going to let us know in advance what you are going to do?"

"Possibly—at times," said the Black Star, smiling. "And I feel sure that this time there will be no little accident that will make it possible for you to take me into custody. By the way, how is your man, Muggs?"

"In excellent condition," Verbeck said.

"My compliments to him, when you see him again, and tell him for me that it will be a pleasure to clash with him. In a way, I admire Muggs. He is such a perfect type of a thug."

"He is not the man to have for an enemy."

"Bah! I could outwit a score of men like Muggs without calling any of my organization to my aid. Well, Mr. Verbeck, I am afraid that we shall have to terminate this interesting conversation. I must get a little rest, and confer with some of my people."

He stepped back to the wall and pressed a button. Immediately the door opened, and the two robed and masked men entered the room. One of them held a vapor gun in his hand.

Roger Verbeck was well aware that it would be a losing fight, yet he fought to his utmost. But the fumes were discharged, the pungent odor struck into his nostrils and filled his lungs, he was forced to gasp for breath—and unconsciousness claimed him.

The last thing he heard was the sarcastic laughter of the Black Star!

CHAPTER IV

OVER THE TELEPHONE

The chief of police, notified by Sheriff Kowen that the Black Star had been rescued cleverly by members of his band, dressed quickly and hurried to police headquarters, there to go into his private office and rave and fume, and relate to the world that Sheriff Kowen was an official who knew not the meaning of precaution and efficiency.

"That's what he gets for being a bug on raiding gambling joints!" the chief cried. "Anybody would have known it was a plant—anybody with brains. We fight that fiend of a Black Star for more than a year, Roger Verbeck finally lands him, we convict the brute and have him handed a stiff sentence—and then an idiotic sheriff allows him to escape! Now I suppose we are in for another reign of terror, with every newspaper in town telling the dear public that the police are fit candidates for some old lady's home!"

There was a lot more of this, while captains and lieutenants, sergeants and roundsmen held their peace and hoped that their superior would not make this an occasion for reprimanding them for some fancied mistake. The chief had worked his way up from the ranks; he was endowed with more brute force than intelligence, and he was a bad man when aroused.

"Call Roger Verbeck's apartment, and get him on the wire!" the chief commanded.

The desk sergeant tried it immediately. He reported that the apartment house did not answer. The chief made a few remarks about sleeping telephone operators, and ordered the desk sergeant to try again. Not getting a reply immediately, the chief called two detectives, ordered them to hurry to Verbeck's place and acquaint him with the news, and to have Verbeck get in communication with the chief at once.

"The first thing the Black Star will do, will be to get hold of Verbeck!" the chief declared. "He'll probably put Verbeck out of the way if we don't prevent it. Verbeck caught him before, and he'll have to do it again. I've got a police force composed of idiots, imbeciles and blockheads! They couldn't catch a turtle walking across the street!"

* * * *

At about the same moment the chief of police was indulging in this tirade, Muggs groaned, tried to turn over and found that he could not, experienced nausea, wondered whether he was being taken down with some disease—and then made the discovery that he was bound and gagged and lashed to the bed.

Having made that discovery, Muggs forced himself to breathe normally, composed himself, and tried to think. The last he remembered, he had retired, started to fall asleep, and had dropped into the middle of a not unpleasant dream. Now it appeared that there had been violence, and he had known nothing of it.

"Burglars!" Muggs thought at first. "Doped while I slept, and tied up like this! I wonder if the boss—"

The mere thought that something disastrous might have happened to Roger Verbeck moved Muggs to instant action. He struggled with his bonds, and at first believed that they could not be slipped; but finally he found a knot that gave a trifle, and he redoubled his efforts, working in a frenzy, his imagination picturing Roger Verbeck robbed and slain.

After a time the knot gave, and Muggs managed to get his hands free. He removed the gag and started working at the cords about his ankles.

"Boss! Boss!" he called.

There came no answer from Verbeck's room. Muggs managed

to get off the last rope, and sprang from the bed. Immediately he reeled and fell back again.

"I'm—sick!" Muggs gasped weakly. "That was—some dope! I wonder what it—"

And then it came to him.

"I know that feelin' in my head and that taste in my mouth!" he told himself. "Vapor gun! I've had enough doses of it before to know! The—the Black Star—"

But the Black Star was safe in a cell in the county jail, and due to be taken to the penitentiary in a few hours, Muggs tried to tell himself. However, Muggs did not have a lot of faith in jails, having escaped from them twice himself before Roger Verbeck saved his life and made a man of him.

Once more he started to get up from the bed, this time slowly and cautiously. He did not experience the nausea now, and though he still felt weak, yet he managed to stagger across the room toward the door.

He went into Verbeck's bedchamber and snapped on the lights. Verbeck was not there. The room was in confusion. Verbeck's clothes, that Muggs had put out for use in the morning, were gone, and his pajamas were on the floor in a corner.

Muggs hurried to the bed. It was there, pasted on the head-piece—a tiny black star!

"If he hurt my boss—" Muggs began, almost sobbing.

And then he felt moved to sudden action again. He rushed into the living room and to the telephone. He rattled the hook frantically, and presently heard the operator's reply.

"I want the police!" Muggs cried into the transmitter. "Mr. Verbeck is gone—been taken away!"

"Say! There are a couple of detectives here now to see Mr. Verbeck," the operator replied. "They're coming right up!"

Muggs darted back into his own room and began dressing with such speed that he was almost fully clothed when the officers knocked at the door. Muggs hurried to let them in.

"What's this about Mr. Verbeck?" one of them asked.

"The Black Star's got him!" Muggs cried. "They doped us while we slept, and—"

"I guess I can tell you all about that," the detective interrupted. "They put out the night clerk and the telephone operator with those cursed vapor guns."

"And Mr. Verbeck is gone! They must have taken him! We've got to find him! There's a black star—pasted on his bed—"

"The chief just sent us up to see Verbeck about this business. The Black Star's gang rescued their leader tonight—turned him loose. He left a note saying that he was going to raid the town."

"Well, why stand here and gas about it?" Muggs demanded. "Don't you understand that the Black Star's got my boss? He put the big crook in jail before, and you can probably guess what he'll get handed to him for it now, if the Black Star is loose!"

"Well, what can we do?" one of the detectives asked. "All we found out was that there was a closed auto out in front, and three or four men with it. If they carried Verbeck away, it's a wild guess where they took him. This town has some size, remember, and the Black Star and his gang are smooth customers."

"You're a fine lot of detectives!" Muggs sneered. "You don't know what to do, huh? Expect to find him by standin' around here smokin' cheap cigars? Why don't you talk to headquarters and tell what you know? Get busy!"

One of the detectives called the station and made his report to the chief. The police reporters were electrified by the statement that Roger Verbeck had been abducted by members of the master crook's organization. At the time the Black Star was arrested, he had sworn to have vengeance on Verbeck, and though he claimed that he abhorred violence, and seldom resorted to it, there were fears and misgivings lest Verbeck's body be found in some lonely spot, a black star pasted on the forehead.

The chief had not been idle. Every officer in the city was

alert. The police knew that the master criminal must have a headquarters somewhere, and that it was their duty to locate it. Until he was under arrest again, and his band broken up, he was a constant menace. He was liable to strike at any part of the city, at any moment of day or night. The blow might fall upon one of the big banks, or upon some social gathering where a fortune in jewels could be obtained.

News of Verbeck's abduction was flashed to all officers as soon as possible. Roads leading from the city were under guard, and all vehicles were being stopped and their occupants questioned. Arrangements had been made to quiz real estate and rental firms in the morning, ascertain every recent lease, and investigate it. The chief had given out word that the headquarters of the master criminal had to be found, and without delay.

Muggs journeyed to headquarters with the two detectives, and told all that he knew. And then he paced the chief's private office, raging, begging them to do something, to give him only as much as a clew regarding where Roger Verbeck had been taken, and he, Muggs, would rescue him alone.

In vain the chief attempted to quiet Muggs.

"He's my boss—he ain't yours!" Muggs shrieked. "He saved my life and he showed me how to make a man of myself! Maybe you don't care what becomes of him, but I do. And if that big crook harms him, I'll get Mr. Black Star if it takes me the rest of my life, and I'll choke the life out of him with my bare hands!"

"Muggs, we're doing all that we can!" the chief protested.

"What are you doin'? Yellin' over the telephone to a bunch of cops and havin' them run around in circles?"

"But we can't do anything else!" the chief cried. "All we can do is—"

The bell of his telephone rang. The chief whirled around and took down the receiver.

"Hello!" he cried.

"Hello!" a man's voice answered. "Well, well, it is some time since I had the pleasure of speaking to you over a telephone wire, chief."

"Who is this?" the chief cried. "We're pretty busy here tonight, and—"

"I suppose that is all my fault. Don't you recognize my voice? I am the Black Star!"

"Oh, are you?" the chief shouted. "Well, you put one over on Sheriff Kowen, but we'll pick you up before long!"

"You think so?" the Black Star asked, laughing.

"I know it, you crook! We'll get you, and we'll get the men and women of that gang of yours!"

"Well, well! You are talking violently, chief—but you always were inclined to violence."

"I'll be violent enough when I get my hands on you, all right!"

"And I just called you up to give you some information. Are you concerned about Roger Verbeck? One of my men reported a few minutes ago that you were. You see, I am keeping in touch with you, chief. I know every order you issue, every plan you make."

"What about Verbeck?"

"Don't worry about him. I had him taken to my headquarters so I could have a little conversation with him. Half an hour ago he was dropped, drugged, and unconscious, at the edge of one of the city parks. No doubt he will be with you soon."

"Your headquarters, huh?" the chief cried. "We'll locate that little place within twenty-four hours, if it is in the city!"

"You think so? I assure you that it is in the city—and perhaps in a quarter where you'd least expect to find it. I scarcely think you can find it inside twenty-four hours, chief. Besides, you are going to be very busy before then."

"I am, eh?"

"You are," the Black Star said. "You will be wondering how

we did it."

"Did what?"

"What it is that we are going to do—the first blow, chief!"

"Lost your nerve, have you? You used to tell us what you were going to do, and dare us to catch you at it."

"Chief, your work is too coarse. Trying to anger me into telling you my plans, are you? It cannot be done tonight, chief. But I'll tell you this much—we intend making quite a haul! Expenses have been heavy recently, you know, and I must have a sort of indemnity."

"You'll get something worse than that when we get our hands on you!" the exasperated chief cried. "You'll go up for life when we catch you!"

"Catch me first!" the Black Star suggested. "By the way, some of my men left Muggs bound and gagged when they carried Verbeck away. You should see that he is released."

"He has been—he's here."

Muggs thrust the chief aside and grasped the receiver.

"Yes, he's here, you big crook!" Muggs cried. "He'll be on hand when you're caught, too, and then you want to look out for yourself! Kidnap my boss, will you?"

"Why, Muggs, how violent you are!"

"You—you—" Muggs sputtered. "When I get hold of you, I'll make you think you never saw or heard tell of that violence stuff before! I'll show you some real violence, you crook!"

"Tut, tut, Muggs! You'll be working yourself into a passion, my dear boy. By the way, Muggs, tell the chief that he need not bother about tracing this telephone call. I have tapped a private wire and am talking over it—understand?"

A click came over the wire, and it went dead. Muggs put up the receiver and turned away from the desk, growling.

The door of the office was thrown open—and Roger Verbeck

hurried in.

"Boss! Boss!" Muggs cried.

"One minute, Muggs! We haven't time for a demonstration of affection at present. Well, chief, he had me nabbed, and I've seen the inside of his new headquarters."

"Know where they are?"

"I haven't the slightest idea. I was in an inside room—unconscious when taken there, and unconscious when they brought me away. I came back to life up in the park, where they had dropped me, got a taxi and hurried here. I suppose we have it all to do over again. We've got to catch that fiend, of course!"

"Will you help, Verbeck?" the chief cried. "Will you take the time and trouble?"

"You know it! Why, the Black Star challenged me again—said I couldn't catch him."

"You're in command, Verbeck, as you were the other time. Any orders now? Where shall we start in?"

"You're having the roads watched?"

"Of course."

"Throw out the dragnet and pick up what you can. Can't tell—might get a clew of some sort, you know. Get the rental agencies—"

"I've planned to do that."

"It probably will do no good, but it won't hurt any to try. The Black Star is too smooth to be caught in that way. His headquarters probably is in some house one of his band has owned and occupied for years."

"He just called up," Muggs put in. "He said we'd be busy within twenty-four hours."

"And the Black Star, as we know well, always keeps his word!" Roger Verbeck declared. "So his message probably means that he will strike his first blow tomorrow night—or, rather, tonight. But where? And what? Those are the questions."

"And all we can do—" the chief began.

"Is to wait until he strikes, and then take up the trail," Roger Verbeck added. "I found out one thing—he has some new people in his organization. He is using the blackboards again."

"What's that?" the chief asked.

"Each member of the band has a number and a countersign. Each enters the headquarters room robed and masked, and carries on the conversation by means of the blackboards. The Black Star issues his orders the same way. He handles them by number, and in his other organization the numbers were issued by one of his lieutenants."

"What's the use of all that?" the chief asked.

"It is very simple, chief. The Black Star may know what Number Eight or Number Ten does, but he doesn't know the identities of the persons with those numbers. He never could go on the witness stand and swear that a certain member of his band did a certain share of the work. Understand? It is a protection all around. On the other hand, the men could not swear that the Black Star issued the orders—it might be somebody else wearing the master crook's robe and mask. See?"

"He's a clever devil!" the chief grunted.

"He is!" Verbeck agreed. "We discovered that much before, remember. But we know his methods now, and that is a help. We will not make the mistake of underestimating him. It's all right to let him think so, and to talk like it when he calls up by telephone, but in truth we know we're up against a tough proposition, and we've got to act accordingly."

"You mean to say you think it's going to be a hard job landing him?" the chief asked.

"I mean just that," said Roger Verbeck. "But we'll get him!"

"You can bet we will!" added Mr. Muggs.

CHAPTER V

TRAILED

The morning newspapers had some very uncomplimentary things to say, both in the news columns and on the editorial page, concerning Sheriff Kowen.

The sheriff, who had had less than three hours' sleep, raged when he read, and tore the papers into shreds.

"That's right—blame me!" he shrieked. "Blame a man who was trying to do his duty! If I don't raid gambling houses, I get blamed, and if I do raid 'em, I get blamed again. How did I know that place was a plant? It was a gambling house, wasn't it?"

Since the sheriff was a bachelor, there was nobody in his apartment to enjoy this tirade. He went to his favorite restaurant for breakfast, and sat at a table far back in one corner, refusing to hold conversation with anybody who approached.

The sheriff was gathering anger. He did not intend to let Roger Verbeck and the police get all the credit when the master crook was caught again. He would go after the Black Star himself, he decided—swear in more deputies and call upon his men to win. There were certain political reasons for this. Moreover, the sheriff was a conscientious man; since the Black Star had escaped through his work, it was his duty, he felt, to recapture him.

Sheriff Kowen left the restaurant and walked toward the county jail, where he maintained his office. He passed countless persons he knew, both men and women, and saw many smiles that possessed a quality the sheriff did not relish. But he refused to take a taxicab—he would show the public that he was not in hiding!

"If I ever meet that Blanchard woman again—" the sheriff told himself; and just then he saw her.

She was on the walk a few feet ahead of him, going slowly toward a department store. Sheriff Kowen hurried up to her, touched her on the arm.

"I want to talk to you!" he said gruffly.

"Oh, good morning, sheriff!" she said, and smiled.

The sheriff was disconcerted for an instant, but composure returned to him quickly.

"We are only a block from the jail, and my office," he said. "I want to talk to you there. Shall we walk, or shall I call a cab and charge it to the county?"

There was a certain meaning to the last sentence, but she did not seem to realize it.

"I should be charmed to talk to you," she said, "but I have some shopping to do this morning."

"Your shopping will have to wait, young woman. This is a serious business."

"Why, what can you mean?" she asked.

"Either you walk along with me to my office, or you go as a prisoner!"

"Are you insane? Arrest me?"

"In a minute!" said Sheriff Kowen.

"I—I don't understand this—but I'll go along with you," said Mamie Blanchard.

"I thought you would," the sheriff returned.

He said nothing more as they walked down the street. He took her into his private office and offered her a chair at one end of his desk. He closed the door, telling the stenographer that he was not to be disturbed for the present.

"Now kindly tell me the meaning of this," said Mamie

Blanchard. "I—you almost frightened me!"

"What do you know about the Black Star?" Kowen asked.

"Why, I read this morning that he escaped from your jail last night. You should be more careful."

Sheriff Kowen's face turned purple with wrath, but he controlled himself and bent toward her across the desk.

"And the cell he formerly occupied is now empty," he said. "Are you anxious to inhabit it for a time?"

"What do you mean, sir?" asked Mamie Blanchard.

"You tipped me off about that gambling house. It was nothing more or less than a trap whereby the Black Star could get a gang of his men into the jail and free him. You know it, and I know it, and it won't do you any good to try to bluff me!"

"Why, how dare you? How perfectly silly!"

"Silly, is it?"

"I never heard of such a thing! This affair must have turned your brain! I came in here yesterday merely to ask you if you required the services of a woman detective. I always have wanted to take up detective work, you know. You told me you did not, and so I left."

"What sort of nonsense is this?" the sheriff cried.

"Nonsense? Oh, I am sorry now that there was nobody else in the office to hear me!" And Miss Mamie Blanchard sat back and smiled at the official on the other side of the desk.

"So that's the way of it!" Kowen said. "You'll stick to that story, will you, because nobody else heard what you said yesterday? Woman detective! You know what you came in here for yesterday—to carry out the orders of the Black Star, help frame up that gambling-house deal—"

"Really, I do not care to listen to any more such talk!" Mamie Blanchard told him. "I am living with my mother at a respectable private hotel—"

"And your brother, the one who was going to the dogs?"

"Oh, I have no brother! You must be mistaken, sir!"

"You told me yesterday—"

"Really, you are mistaken. You are confusing my conversation with that of some other person, surely. Brother? Oh, no, sir!"

Sheriff Kowen stared at her. "You are a wonder," he said, "but I am afraid that you can't get away with it. The best thing for you will be tell me all you know about the Black Star, where his headquarters are located, and what he has planned to do. Do that—and do it right—and I may forget all about what happened yesterday."

"But I do not understand you! How should I know anything about that notorious criminal."

"Want me to throw you into that empty cell?"

"You dare!" she said, indignantly. "My people have money, sir, and I can promise you a damage suit that will give you food for thought! Are you not ridiculous enough in the eyes of the public already?"

Sheriff Kowen's face purpled again as he glared at her. He did not doubt, knowing the past history of the Black Star's organization, that this Blanchard woman would cause him trouble.

"Well, I'm going to let you get away with it for the time being," he said. "But don't think for a minute that you're fooling me! You are a member of the Black Star's gang, and I know it! When we land him and the others, we'll land you, too! And you'll get a nice, long sentence from the court!"

Mamie Blanchard stood up. "I do not care to be insulted further!" she said. "I regret that there are no witnesses. If you annoy me any more, I shall bring the matter to my lawyer's attention."

"I suppose he belongs to the gang also," said the sheriff.

He got up, too, but before he did, he touched a button beneath his desk. It caused a buzzer to sound in another office. This told the deputy there that the person leaving the sheriff's private room was to be shadowed.

Kowen opened the door and bowed his visitor out. She held her head high, and there was an expression of indignation in her face. The sheriff watched her disappear into the hall, and then reached for his hat.

On second thought, Kowen had decided to shadow Mamie Blanchard himself, assisting his deputy. He gave Miss Blanchard time to reach the street, and then he started. She was already half a block away, making for the nearest department store, and Kowen saw his faithful deputy trailing her.

Mamie Blanchard, under the eyes of the sheriff and deputy, entered the store and began making purchases in an ordinary manner. Kowen approached the deputy and engaged him in low conversation.

"That's the girl that tipped me off about the gambling house," he said, "and I know blamed well that she belongs to the Black Star's gang. I tried to get some information out of her just now, but she's pretty wise. We'll keep out of her sight, work independently, and trail her. She may lead us to the big crook's headquarters."

Mamie Blanchard made purchases at several departments, and then left the store. If she was aware that she was under surveillance, she did not betray it by her actions. She visited a soda fountain and ate ice cream, emerged again, and finally engaged a taxicab. Sheriff Kowen engaged another, and his deputy a third.

They trailed her to a part of the city where were to be found houses that once had been the homes of wealthy persons of social prominence. But now those of wealth and society had moved to another section, and these relics of other days were rented for various purposes. Here were to be found small shops, cheap boarding houses, palmists, clairvoyants and others of their ilk.

Here and there were smaller houses back from the street, some with billboards before them.

Mamie Blanchard left her taxicab at a corner, glanced around, and walked down the street. Kowen and the deputy shadowed her. It was not difficult in this section.

Mamie Blanchard was acting as if apprehensive now. She glanced around continually. Once she stood for several minutes in front of a store window.

"On the right track!" Sheriff Kowen told himself. "She's going to that crook's headquarters, all right, and she wants to make sure she isn't being followed."

He made a sign to his deputy, and they began to approach each other. Mamie Blanchard had walked on down the street. Suddenly she darted through a little gate, and walked swiftly toward one of the smaller houses that sat back from the street.

Kowen and his deputy saw her go into the cottage.

"Go telephone for half a dozen of the men," Kowen ordered the other. "When they come, scatter them around the block, and then come back here to me. Either that house is the Black Star's headquarters, or the people there have something to do with him. I'll watch."

The deputy hurried away, and Kowen kept his eyes on the house. He supposed there was a rear door, but behind the house was a high, blank wall, and he knew that nobody could leave the place without walking directly toward him.

Kowen's heart began pounding at his ribs. If he could capture the Black Star so soon after his escape, he would be the man of the hour. He would show charity by calling in the police and Roger Verbeck, but theirs would be reflected glory, and Kowen knew it well.

The deputy returned at the end of half an hour. Men were posted behind the alley wall, he explained, and were watching the house from the buildings on either side. Nobody could get out without being seen and stopped.

"Then we'll go in," the sheriff said.

They walked boldly to the front door of the cottage, and the sheriff rang the bell. Nobody answered. Three times he rang, and yet nobody came to the door, nor could they hear the slightest sound inside the house.

"They're in there, all right; and won't answer!" Sheriff Kowen whispered to the deputy. "They have spotted us, and know that we have them cornered. I'm going to signal for the other men, and we'll break into the place. It's stretching the law a little, maybe, but I'll run the risk. This isn't like an ordinary case; we're after the Black Star, remember!"

The sheriff gave the signal, and then he and the deputy remained on guard and alert for five minutes, at the end of which time half a dozen more deputies had come from near-by buildings and joined their superior officer. Kowen explained the situation to them in a few words.

"And you want to be ready to go into action!" he concluded. "If the Black Star or any of his gang are in this house, they'll be prepared to put up a fight, and don't forget it! Watch out for those vapor guns and bombs!"

The sheriff rang the bell again, waited for several minutes, gave those inside a last chance to come to the door. But he waited in vain.

"Can't afford to waste any more time," he told his men. "We saw that Blanchard woman go in there, and, from the way she acted before she did, I'm sure this is either the big crook's head-quarters or where some of his people are living. Every minute we wait out here, we give them a chance to get ready for us. Two of you men remain outside and see that nobody gets away from the place; I'll call you if we need you inside."

Kowen signaled to one of his biggest deputies. The man

advanced, put his shoulder against the door, pressed against it.

"Got it bolted, I guess!" he said.

He backed away, rushed forward, struck the door again with his shoulder, and burst the door open.

Sheriff Kowen and his deputies sprawled into the little front hall of the cottage!

CHAPTER VI

WHAT KOWEN FOUND

No volley greeted them.

There was no crash of vapor bombs, no cloud of pungent gas, no clash with desperate and determined criminals who fought on behalf of their leader and master!

There was nothing but silence—a silence broken only by the deep breathing of the sheriff and his deputies, who had sprawled into that hall expecting to meet with instant battle, and to whom the unexplained silence was more trying than combat.

Again Sheriff Kowen gave a signal, and one of the men opened the door at the end of the hall. They entered an ordinary living room that was adorned with cheap furniture; it might have been the living room of the home of a family in moderate circumstances.

They passed on to a small dining room, investigating an ordinary bedchamber. Sheriff Kowen began thinking that he had made a serious mistake.

"That woman came in here—and where is she now?" the sheriff said. "Search the rest of the house—go into the basement—don't leave a corner untouched. We're in here now, and we might as well do our work. That woman is here some place, remember that. We saw her come in, and she hasn't left."

They searched the kitchen, another small bedroom, and found nothing, neither a trace of Mamie Blanchard nor anything that would indicate that the cottage was a den of thieves. They located a trap door, and opened it, and saw a flight of steps running down into a dark basement.

"Careful!" Kowen warned his men. "They're probably down

there waiting for us! We'll not all run into the trap!"

He delegated one man to remain above. He flashed his electric torch, but could see nothing except the flight of steps and the landing at the bottom. With some of the others close behind him, with his electric torch in one hand and his revolver in the other, Sheriff Kowen started to descend the steps.

Each instant they expected to hear the sound of a shot, or the explosion of a vapor bomb, or to encounter one of the traps rumor said the Black Star always had in his headquarters. Step by step they descended, but nothing happened.

They reached the landing, peered around the corner of a concrete projection. Sheriff Kowen gasped.

"Careful!" he warned again. "This is the headquarters, all right, and there doesn't seem to be anybody here—but you never can tell. Watch out for tricks and traps! Be careful what you touch and where you step. When he was after the Black Star before, Roger Verbeck found himself in a trap when he thought he was boss of the situation—don't forget that!"

The sheriff stepped to the floor, walked a couple of paces away from the steps. He saw an electric switch on the wall, hesitated a moment, and then turned it. The basement was bathed in light.

All the deputies with him were on the floor of the basement now. A chorus of gasps escaped them.

The basement was not like the rest of the house. It was furnished lavishly. In the middle was a long table. At either end was a blackboard on the wall. There were half a score of heavy chairs scattered about. There were some papers on the table.

"Watch the walls," Kowen instructed. "We've found the new headquarters, all right. We'll beat Roger Verbeck and the police this time, thank Heaven! Watch the walls—they're liable to open up and let a gang of thugs in on us any time. I'm going to look at these papers on the table."

He posted his deputies where he wished them, and advanced

slowly and carefully across the floor. He was afraid the floor would open and swallow him, afraid of some clever trap that would turn victory into defeat and make him a laughingstock.

He reached the table without accident, and glanced at the papers there. There was no handwriting in sight. The papers had been printed with tiny rubber stamps. Kowen remembered that such was the Black Star's method.

He picked up the nearest and began reading. His eyes bulged and an exclamation escaped him.

"Great—great!" he muttered.

For he was holding in his hands some of the master rogue's orders to his band. Moreover, they had to do with the campaign of crime the Black Star had promised. Kowen read it swiftly:

> Number Eleven reports that all is in readiness in his department. Number Four will be at his post a quarter of an hour before midnight. Number Ten will have charge of the men opening the vault. One of the watchmen is a man of ours and will attend to his companion; he is to be bound and gagged afterward by Number Eight, as we may need him again and do not want any suspicion attached to him. Automobiles will be at either end of the alley. Exit through basement door after work is done. The bags of gold are to be put in the limousine, which will be driven by Number Twenty.

"This is great!" Kowen told himself again. "If we only can nab the whole gang—"

He picked up another sheet of paper, and started reading that. Once more an exclamation of satisfaction escaped him.

Midnight, Tuesday. National Trust Company. Preliminary work completed. All who have received orders will act accordingly. Must be no failure in this first case. Loot will be heavy.

"Going to tap the National Trust, is he?" Sheriff Kowen said. "Well, we'll be ready for him at midnight! He's going to run into a bunch of trouble."

The chief deputy stepped to his side. "Suppose they find out that we have located their headquarters," he said.

"Let us hope they won't find it out," replied the sheriff. "Don't touch another thing here."

"How about that woman?"

"That's the one thing that puzzles me," the sheriff admitted. "She came in here, and we didn't see her leave, and I don't see where she can be. I suppose she came to get orders, or something like that."

"You can bet that there's some other way to get out of here," the deputy told him. "You can bet that the Black Star doesn't let his gang hang around headquarters much. The way he did before was to have them show up one or two at a time, at certain intervals. He's probably issued all his orders and has quit for the day."

One of the other deputies startled them.

"Here's a little trap door—and a tunnel!" he said.

Sheriff Kowen hurried to the corner. The deputy had spoken the truth. There was a small trap door in the floor, and when it was opened the mouth of a narrow tunnel was disclosed. Sheriff Kowen issued his orders rapidly. Into the tunnel they went, flashing their electric torches, revolvers held ready for instant use.

They followed it a distance of a hundred feet—a dusty tunnel that twisted like a serpent. They came to another small door, finally managed to get it open—and stepped through the thick wall into the alley!

"So that is it!" the sheriff exclaimed. "That is how the woman got away from the house without our seeing her! Careful, now! We'll go back and see that everything is as we found it. I've got a little plan that will be a winner!"

Back they went through the tunnel. They closed the door, saw that the rugs were in place and that everything in the basement was as it should be, and went up the flight of steps.

They made sure that nothing in the house had been disturbed, went outside, and found that the front door had not been much damaged. One of the deputies locked and bolted it on the inside, then got out through a window.

"We'll hope that none of his gang has seen us around here," the sheriff explained. "I've got to let the police in on this, but we'll get the credit, all right. I haven't men enough! We'll have deputies and police scattered all around this place tonight, and we'll nab anybody that goes into this cottage, either by the front door or the alley tunnel. We'll be waiting for Mr. Black Star at the National Trust Company's place, too. The police can help, but we'll get the credit! And when we get that crook back in jail—"

Sheriff Kowen did not finish the sentence, but some of his deputies grinned. They realized that the master crook would be in for a bad hour when he was once more behind the bars. Sheriff Kowen knew how to punish prisoners who tried to escape.

"The big crook isn't as clever as he was before," the sheriff said. "I guess those few months in jail have dulled his wits. If we can catch some of those whelps that worked the game on us and got him away, I'll be highly gratified. I won't need much help when it comes to teaching them a lesson!"

Once more his deputies grinned. They walked to the corner, received fresh orders there, and scattered. Sheriff Kowen engaged a taxicab and ordered the chauffeur to take him to police headquarters with the greatest possible speed, traffic regulations notwithstanding.

He found the chief of police there, and Roger Verbeck in conference with him. Verbeck's big roadster was at the curb, and Muggs was at the wheel. Kowen grinned at him as he entered the building.

"So here you are!" the chief greeted him. "You've got a nerve to show your face after letting the Black Star get away from you!"

"Oh, I don't know!" Kowen said, smiling at them. "Have you gentlemen done anything?"

"What can we do except wait until he pulls off a stunt, and then go after him?" the chief demanded.

"Go after him first! That is what I did."

"Oh, did you?" asked the chief mildly.

"With some measure of success," said the sheriff modestly. "I have discovered the Black Star's headquarters. I have seen some orders to his gang that he left scattered around his table. I found nobody at home when I called, and have every reason to believe that the crook and his gang don't know they have been located."

"Where is the place?" Verbeck asked.

The sheriff told him.

"Possibly you are right," Verbeck said. "But the Black Star is a tricky individual, remember. And the orders are—"

"At midnight tonight," said Sheriff Kowen, trying to retain his modesty, "the Black Star's gang will try to loot the National Trust Company's vaults. Now, let's get down to business!"

CHAPTER VII

VERBECK INVESTIGATES

Roger Verbeck and the chief looked at the sheriff aghast. His announcement had startled them. In his previous career of crime, the master criminal had raided that establishment, and had almost wrecked it because he removed so many assets.

"How do you know that, Kowen?" the chief demanded.

The sheriff told the story, not sparing himself, for he wanted to convince the men before him, and now that the recapture of the Black Star seemed so near, he could afford to speak the truth.

He related the story of Mamie Blanchard's first visit to his office, and of how he had trailed her after meeting her on the street.

"That woman," said Verbeck, after Kowen had described her carefully, "is a member of the old organization, and is known as The Princess. She caused us a lot of trouble before."

"She certainly did!" the chief admitted. "She is almost as clever as the Black Star, is trusted by him, and handles a lot of his work. We didn't get her when we caught the Black Star and smashed his old gang, and we had supposed that she had left the country—possibly had gone to South America. She came from Brazil, originally."

Then Kowen continued his story, and told of finding the papers on the table in the basement.

"That's the part of it I don't like," Verbeck said. "It isn't like the master crook to leave papers like those scattered around."

"Didn't you get into his old headquarters once and find papers and orders there?" the sheriff demanded.

"I did, I'll admit. But really I do not like the appearance of this. Describe that basement room to me again, Kowen."

The sheriff did so.

"Well, you seem to have described the room I saw last night," Roger Verbeck said. "Perhaps you are right; but I think we are assuming too much when we think the Black Star's people are not aware of the visit of you and your men there. It would be more like him to have the place watched continually."

"It all looks good to me," the chief put in. "I happen to know that the National Trust Company has a lot of gold in its vault just now—and you can bet that the Black Star knows it, too. That organization of his is a wonder. Why, my own secretary might belong to it, for all I know. We found a police captain in the old one, remember."

"Well, what are we going to do about it?" the sheriff asked.

"What have you to suggest? It's your game," the chief reminded him.

"I've got to have the help of the police, of course," Kowen replied. "I haven't men enough, and this job calls for trained men. I think we should combine forces."

"Certainly," the chief agreed.

"We ought to have a gang around the block that contains that cottage, ready to nab anybody that goes in or comes out; and we ought to be ready for the crook and his gang at the National Trust."

"How do you want to work it?" the chief asked. "Do you want to watch the cottage with your men?"

"I'll send some of my men there, and you do the same," Kowen replied. "And we'll both have men around the bank. I want to be there when the big row comes off. Let's figure it out!"

"Mr. Verbeck is in command of this, as far as I am concerned," the chief informed him.

"That suits me," the sheriff replied.

They spent an hour perfecting their plans, and then the chief began issuing his orders. Those orders went to officers in all parts of the city. They were of such a nature that the Black Star, if some confederate reported them to him, would not be exactly sure what they meant, except that the chief of police expected him to attempt some gigantic crime and would have his men in readiness.

"If you see that Blanchard woman again, put her in the jug!" the chief told the sheriff. "If you are afraid of a suit for damages, turn her over to me. I'm not! She's The Princess, and there is a little charge pending against her right now. Don't forget that."

"If I had arrested her today, I wouldn't have found the crook's headquarters," Kowen retorted. "But I'll nab her if I see her again, all right!"

The sheriff, well pleased with the arrangements that had been made, left police headquarters and hurried to his own office, to give orders to his own men. Kowen was exceedingly well pleased with himself. Even the chief of police, his ancient enemy, admitted that he had done the work. Kowen could see, in fancy, the newspapers of the following morning, with their glowing accounts of how, within twenty-four hours after the Black Star's escape, he had located the crook's headquarters, had learned his plans, and had captured him again and broken up his band. That should be political capital, Sheriff Kowen thought.

He reached his office, called his chief deputy, and gave him instructions. He warned the man that orders should be issued carefully so that the Black Star might not learn what was planned.

"We don't want to let that crook think we are wise to his game," Kowen said. "If he does, he'll simply move his head-quarters and call off this little robbery. Then we'll have to start all over again—and I want to get that man back in a cell before tomorrow. Newspapers and public jump on me, will they? Tomorrow they'll be saying how great I am!"

The chief of police had remained in his office to make

further plans. Roger Verbeck left, and went out to the roadster. He ordered Muggs to drive to a certain corner across the city. That meant that Roger Verbeck had some deep thinking to do, for, when he had not, he drove the big roadster himself. So Muggs, with a thousand questions trembling on his lips, kept silent, though he looked at Verbeck reproachfully now and then.

Muggs reached the corner Verbeck had designated, and glanced around scornfully. Muggs did not favor this section of the city. It reminded him too much of certain quarters of Paris where he had existed in years gone by, when he had been a criminal.

"Wait here," Verbeck said.

"Aw, boss, ain't I in on this?" Muggs protested.

"Want to have the car tagged for being left longer than the law allows on this street?" Verbeck demanded. "If I am not back in twenty minutes, drive around the block and wait on the opposite corner—and keep that up until I do put in an appearance."

"This ain't a sweet end of town," Muggs said.

"Are you feeling a certain amount of alarm for me, Muggs? Have you an idea that I cannot take care of myself, in broad daylight?"

"Aw!" Muggs exclaimed, in huge disgust.

"You'll get plenty of action, Muggs, before this thing is over, if that is what is bothering you," Verbeck said. "What I am going to do just now calls for one man, and only one."

Verbeck walked down the street, and Muggs hunched down behind the wheel and glared at those who passed.

Verbeck turned the first corner and disappeared, as far as Muggs was concerned. He journeyed another block, turned another corner, and so approached the little cottage that Sheriff Kowen had investigated. He walked past it slowly, and glanced at the building. There was no sign of life about it.

Verbeck went on around the block and turned into the alley. He found the little door in the wall, but there appeared to be no way of opening it from the outside. He hurried on through the alley and made his way to the front again. If this was, in reality, the Black Star's headquarters, Verbeck did not want to spoil things by having some of the band see him loitering in the neighborhood.

He returned to the roadster, told Muggs to drive him home, and grinned at the look of disgust in Muggs' face.

"Ain't I in on this at all, boss?" Muggs wanted to know. "Gee! When we was after that big crook before, you let me know everything. Don't you trust me no more?"

"Certainly I trust you!" Verbeck told him. "You know that I do! But why bother you with minor details? In other words, Muggs, I am not sure of anything yet."

Reaching his rooms, Roger Verbeck spent the remainder of the day reading books, as if the Black Star and his band did not exist and call for thought. He ordered dinner earlier than usual, and then dressed in a plain dark suit, and put on a soft cap.

"Into the roadster again, old boy," he told Muggs. "Drive me to the same corner."

Muggs did so gladly; but when the corner was reached, he was disgusted once more to find that Verbeck wanted him to remain with the car.

"I don't seem to be nothin' but a chauffeur," he complained to the world at large. "I used to amount to somethin', but I guess I don't any more."

"Muggs, I told you that this is a one-man job," Verbeck said. "And I am the one man!"

He walked on down the street, chuckling at Muggs' grumbling. He passed the little cottage once more. There seemed to be no lights inside it. The yard about it was in pitch darkness, for the glare of the street lights was cut off by the high buildings on either side, by the billboards in front and the alley wall behind.

Verbeck slipped inside the yard. For a time he stood against the billboard and listened, and then he went forward like a shadow, and finally reached a corner of the cottage.

He made his way around the building, listening at doors and windows. He found a window unlatched, and raised it inch by inch, without making the slightest noise. A moment later, Roger Verbeck was inside the house.

He held his electric torch ready, and his automatic. Not a sound reached his ears to indicate the presence of any other human being in the house. Verbeck flashed the torch, located a door, passed through it, and was in the kitchen.

There he found the door leading to the basement, and listened beside it for some time. Then he opened it, slowly, cautiously, a bit at a time. There was no light in the basement.

Verbeck propped the door open with a chair, and descended the steps carefully, not flashing his torch. He reached the bottom, listened for some time, and then pressed the button. The shaft of light flashed across the room.

"Kowen was right—this is the place!" Verbeck told himself. "The furniture—everything seems to be the same. But I don't like it. It doesn't seem right, at all. I never knew the Black Star to be careless like this before."

Verbeck flashed his electric torch again and looked carefully around the room. He even walked across to the table and read the orders Sheriff Kowen had found there. The house was being watched by the police and deputies by this time, Verbeck knew, for the men had received orders to take up their positions soon after nightfall. The officers could be depended upon to capture anybody who visited the cottage.

Verbeck went back up the steps, crept through the house, and got out through the window by which he had entered, and which he now closed again. As he moved away from the house, an officer spoke to him.

"I thought that was you, Mr. Verbeck," he said. "Have you

been inside?"

"Yes. There is nobody there now," Verbeck replied. "Is the door in the alley wall being watched?"

"Yes, sir," said the officer. "We've got good men scattered all around the place. If that big crook or any of his people come near here, they'll be nabbed!"

Verbeck hurried up the street and sprang into the roadster, smiling at Muggs' sour look.

"Drive to police headquarters, Muggs," he directed. "We'll stay there until a little before midnight, and then we'll go to the National Trust Company with the chief and his men, and watch for the Black Star. If he really attempts to rob that place tonight, he is going to be caught in the act."

"I'd like to get my two hands on him!" Muggs growled.

"Perhaps you'll have the chance," Verbeck said.

"If I do," Muggs said, "you can bet that the big crook will have a sore throat for a month!"

CHAPTER VIII

MYSTERY AND AN ALARM

Muggs drove the powerful roadster slowly through the streets. The newsboys were crying extra editions of the evening papers, editions that had a great deal in them concerning the master crook and his intentions. Verbeck had Muggs stop, and bought the papers, and was glad to see that there was no inkling of Kowen's discovery in them.

Verbeck did not feel satisfied. Remembering the Black Star's methods, he could not convince himself that the master rogue would let himself be captured again just as he inaugurated his campaign of crime. If the National Trust Company was to be robbed, the Black Star would be there in person, unless he had changed his tactics, for previously he always had commanded his men during a big crime.

But even the greatest criminals are wrecked by trivial accidents, Verbeck knew well, and so he tried to tell himself that it was a careless woman member of the band who had betrayed the crook's headquarters and plans. Yet it was foreign to the character of The Princess, as Mamie Blanchard was called by the members of the organization, to be careless.

"Well, we'll know the truth soon!" Roger Verbeck told himself.

They reached police headquarters and went inside. The chief was waiting for them.

"Everything ready!" he announced. "We're going to land that crook quick this time! I'm taking no chances, you can bet! I'll have every available man around the National Trust Company's building. I've got some of them inside right now, and in the adjoining building, and there will be a crowd in the alley and in the streets."

"I went up and took a look at that cottage," Verbeck said.

"So that's what you were up to!" Muggs put in.

"How did it look?" the chief asked.

"Well, I can't swear to it, of course, but that basement room looked like the one where the Black Star had me last night; and the orders Kowen told us about were on the table. I didn't touch them, but I read them."

"Let us hope the crook doesn't get wise to the fact that we are on to him," said the chief.

"The chances are," said Verbeck, "that he had completed his work when Kowen and his men got inside the house, and that the Blanchard woman was the last of the band to visit there today. If the Black Star follows out his usual method, he'll hurry back there after he pulls off the robbery, providing we don't get him at the bank."

"And if he dodges us at the bank, the men will pick him up when he goes back to the cottage—very pretty!" the chief said. "Verbeck, I have an idea that we are going to win tonight. The rogue's good luck has deserted him, that's all."

The chief opened a box of cigars and passed it around. From time to time a sergeant came in to report about men being posted. Now and then some detective telephoned rumors and information he had gathered.

"The streets are jammed," the chief said, after one of these telephone calls. "The blamed newspapers are out with big stories of how the Black Star telephoned them that he would start his campaign of crime at midnight. Well, somebody in the mob might get hurt, but it helps us, in a way. It has been easier for us to get our men placed without some of the crook's gang reporting the fact to him."

"Oh, the chances are that he knows all about it," Verbeck said. "And he probably doesn't care. The Black Star is original, don't forget that. He'll not try to rob that trust company in any usual manner. He'll get into the building with his men in some way we do not expect, and if we're not on guard he'll get out again—with bags of gold. Did you inform the bank officials?"

"Great Scott, no!" gasped the chief. "They'd light up the place, remove the gold, give the whole thing away. We want to catch the Black Star. I'll guarantee that he'll never get away with anything there tonight. You don't seem to have much confidence, Verbeck."

"I haven't," Verbeck admitted. "I fought the Black Star before, you know. I can't make myself think that he will walk into a trap—yet everything seems to point toward it. Well, I'll be going, I guess. It is eleven o'clock now."

Muggs followed him to the curb, and this time Verbeck took the wheel when they got into the roadster. He drove through the city and toward the place where he lived, and, when he was sure that he was not being followed, he circled through the streets and approached the retail section of the city again.

Verbeck parked the roadster several blocks away from the National Trust Company. Then he and Muggs made their way through the crowd in the street, their caps pulled down over their eyes, Verbeck hoping that he would escape recognition.

They went through an alley, and stopped in the darkness just before they reached the other street. The rear of the trust company building was just opposite them.

"A quarter to twelve," Verbeck whispered. "The chief is to meet us here. The sergeants know where he is to be in case he is needed quickly."

"Why not get into the bank building?" Muggs asked. "Are we going to stay here in the alley and let a bunch of policemen do this thing? Gee, boss, ain't we goin' to handle it ourselves?"

"We'll be right on hand, Muggs, if anything starts," Verbeck promised him. "Don't worry about that!"

Five minutes later, the chief found them there.

"Now for the big drama!" the chief whispered. "Everybody

is set and ready. That master criminal, as he calls himself, is due to receive the surprise of his life in a few minutes. I only hope he is on the job himself—glad to nab any of his crowd, of course, but he is the man we want in particular."

"Those orders read 'midnight,'" Verbeck said. "If he carries them out, we haven't long to wait."

"Got an idea he won't carry 'em out?" the chief asked.

"He may know that we are aware of his intention," Verbeck replied. "He isn't fool enough to walk into a trap when he knows where the trap is, you know."

The chief flashed his torch and glanced at his watch.

"Well, it's three minutes of midnight now," he said. "I wonder how he'll try it."

"He certainly will not walk up to the front door and break it down," said Verbeck, chuckling.

"I've got men in the basements of the buildings on both sides of the trust company," the chief said. "If he tries to use a tunnel, he'll find himself caught."

"He came down from the sky on one occasion," Verbeck reminded the chief.

"Look!" Muggs cried.

He had glanced up at the sky as Verbeck spoke, and now was clutching at their sleeves and asking them to look up, too. Far above the city a bright light appeared, a light that traveled in circles. It grew larger and brighter rapidly. It blazed forth like a monster searchlight, and bathed in splendor the building of the National Trust Company.

"Airplane!" Muggs gasped.

"Then he's a long way up in the air," said the chief. "An airplane makes considerable noise! It isn't an airplane!"

"Then what is it?" Verbeck asked.

"You've got me—but it isn't an airplane, or, if it is, it must be a couple of miles high. That light doesn't seem to be that high up."

The crowds in the street were yelling and shrieking now. The searchlight continued to bathe the trust company's building in brilliance. The police and deputies posted around the corner were amazed. Sheriff Kowen, on the other side of the building, ran around like an insane man, calling upon his men to do something.

The light was extinguished; and again it blazed forth, and this time it swept up and down the alley, revealing the chief and Verbeck and Muggs, and officers who had been posted there.

"The Black Star has something to do with that!" the chief said.

"And he's spotted us!" said Verbeck.

"Then we lose, for he'll not try to rob the trust company."

"Don't be too sure of that! Some of his band may be in there now, and this light, wherever it is, may be to attract our attention while other men carry away the loot."

"I've got plenty of men in the building," the chief replied, "and they'll flash a signal the moment they see anybody that doesn't belong in there. That light gets me. How high do you suppose it is?"

"It's comin' closer to the ground," said Muggs.

Once more the light was extinguished, and the crowds in the street grew silent. Again it blazed forth, and this time it was so bright and near that a man could not look into it.

Then they heard a laugh, and the well-known voice of the Black Star.

"Hello, chief! Hello, Verbeck and Muggs! Watching the trust company, are you? I'm afraid that'll not do any good!"

The chief drew his revolver and fired rapidly into the air. The Black Star's sarcastic laugh reached them, and the light was extinguished again. The sky was black; they saw nothing, heard nothing.

"What kind of a thing is this?" the chief gasped. "He wasn't more than a hundred feet above us when he spoke. What can it be? He can't be in an airplane, or we'd hear the roar of the engine!"

"And his band is probably looting the vault of the trust company right now, or has looted it!" Verbeck said.

He ran quickly across the street, and Muggs and the chief followed at his heels. They knocked on a rear door of the building, and it was opened at once.

"Everything all right?" the chief asked.

"Nothing doing yet, chief," replied the detective who had opened the door.

"We'll take a look and make sure," the chief said. "I don't like this business at all!"

They went through a corridor and found the two watchmen. They had the lights in the vault room switched on.

"That vault hasn't been touched," Verbeck said, "unless they have tunneled from beneath. The door hasn't been opened."

"That crook was wise," the chief declared. "He knew that we were here waiting for him. How he found it out is more than I can tell—some of Sheriff Kowen's carelessness, I suppose."

A detective came running toward them through the corridor.

"Chief!" he shrieked. "Sergeant just came from headquarters! He says that the Black Star's gang is looting the First National—just got the alarm!"

CHAPTER IX

ORDERS AND LETTERS

The forces of law and order would have been interested, that day, had they watched Mamie Blanchard continually.

When she entered the little cottage, she locked the door on the inside, hurried through the kitchen and into the basement, and entered the tunnel. She went through it quickly, reached the door in the alley wall, listened, opened it, slipped into the alley, and slammed the door shut again. That door could not be opened from the outside unless a person knew exactly how to do it.

Mamie Blanchard hurried through the alley to the street, engaged a taxicab, and drove to a certain hotel, where she ascended in the elevator and went directly to a suite. It was not the same hotel she had visited after telling Sheriff Kowen about the gambling house, but she found the same people there—a middle-aged woman and a middle-aged man.

"Well?" the man asked gruffly.

"Couldn't be better," said Mamie Blanchard.

"What happened?"

"I let him see me, and he took me to his office in the jail. Said he knew that I was a member of the Black Star's band, and threatened to put me in a cell if I didn't tell all I knew. I bluffed him, of course, and then he got the wise idea of letting me go and trailing me. You could almost see it sticking out on his forehead." Miss Blanchard stopped to laugh.

"Go on!" the man commanded.

"The sheriff and a deputy trailed me. When I got near the cottage, I began acting in a peculiar manner. I hurried inside, locked the door, and went out through the tunnel and the alley.

At the corner, I saw the sheriff and his deputy still looking at the cottage."

"Well, you did your part!" the man said. "Now we'll wait to learn whether the rest of the plan worked out."

They waited for half an hour. Then the telephone rang, and the man answered. When he hung up the receiver and turned away, he was grinning.

"It worked!" he said. "Number Ten has just reported. The sheriff sent for more men, and broke into the house. They found the basement room and read the orders, and they found the tunnel, too. Number Ten reports that the sheriff has gone to police headquarters."

"And that means," said Mamie Blanchard, "that there'll be half a hundred cops around that cottage tonight, and all the rest will be at the National Trust Company."

"Exactly! And while they are at the National Trust, we'll be looting the First National. That fake headquarters did the trick—just as the big boss said it would!"

"What now, Landers?" Miss Blanchard asked.

It was the first time she had spoken his name. Like herself, Landers had been in the Black Star's old organization, and now was one of the master criminal's shrewd lieutenants. He had helped organize the new band, and had engineered the Black Star's rescue.

"I must go and report," he said. "I'll report for you, too. You'd better stay pretty close to this suite for a few days. They'll be looking for you now, you know."

"I might as well be in jail as be a prisoner here," Mamie Blanchard pouted.

"It's orders!" Landers told her. "You'll be needed again soon, and needed badly."

Landers left the hotel, engaged a taxicab, and drove out along the river road until he came to a resort. He paid the chauffeur there, and walked along the shore, watching the bathers, acting like a prosperous man on a little holiday.

But after a time he left the resort and walked on along the road. He turned into a lane, when he was sure that he was not being observed, and approached a ramshackle farmhouse that was hidden in a grove.

Landers entered the house, went down a flight of steps to the basement, and stopped in a little room. There he put on a long black robe and his black mask, and touched a button. In the distance a bell tinkled. Then a buzzer sounded, and Landers opened the door and stepped into the Black Star's headquarters.

The master rogue was sitting at one end of the table. He got up and stepped to the nearest blackboard. Landers went to the one at the other end of the room, and picked up the chalk.

"Number One," he wrote.

"Countersign?" wrote the Black Star.

"Amboy."

"Report!" the Black Star wrote.

Landers turned to the blackboard and wrote rapidly.

"Sheriff decoyed to fake headquarters. Decoy escaped in manner planned. Sheriff broke in and found room in basement. Number Ten reported to me that everything was left as it was, and that sheriff went immediately to police headquarters."

"Good," wrote the Black Star.

"Any further orders?"

"Act tonight in accordance with the orders given you yesterday," the Black Star wrote. "That is all."

Landers bowed, and backed from the room. He took off mask and gown and hung them up, put on his hat and gloves, and made his way from the house and into the lane again. Once more he was the prosperous gentleman enjoying a day in the woods and along the river.

Back in the old farmhouse, the Black Star was receiving

another report, this time by telephone.

"Number Eight," said the voice.

"Countersign?" asked the Black Star.

"Harvard!"

"Well?"

"I have been in communication with Number Twelve, who is in police headquarters. Sheriff Kowen went there and held a conference with the chief and Roger Verbeck. They fell hard for that fake headquarters stunt. They are planning to watch the place tonight, and all officers not there will be in the neighborhood of the National Trust Company, where they expect us to strike."

"Very good!" the Black Star said. "You have your orders for tonight?"

"Yes, sir."

"Carry them out. There is nothing new!"

The master rogue hung up the receiver, put the telephone away in a secret niche in the wall, and sat down at the end of the long table again. A man entered with a tray containing luncheon, and the Black Star removed his mask and ate. The servant was a member of the old organization, and took part in no crimes—it was not necessary for the Black Star to wear a mask in his presence.

Having eaten, the master criminal stretched himself on a couch in one corner of the room, and slept. It was dusk when he awakened. He ate again, and as he finished the little bell on the wall jangled. The Black Star put on his mask, and touched a button.

The robed and masked man who entered was small. He went

directly to the blackboard.

"Number Sixteen," he wrote.

"Countersign?"

"Providence."

"Report!"

"First National received shipment of currency today as expected," the other wrote.

"What amount?"

"Three hundred thousand."

"What else have you to report?"

"One of the watchmen is our man, and he will attend to the other. Number Twenty has investigated the vault, and reports that he can open it in twelve or fifteen minutes."

"How about transportation?" the Black Star wrote.

"One limousine and three closed autos; all has been arranged."

"Good!" the Black Star wrote. "That is all—except I want no mistakes made tonight."

The other man left the room. The master criminal touched a bell button, and the servant entered.

"Has the mechanic reported?" the Black Star asked.

"Yes, sir. The machine is in perfect working order, sir. He will test it further after dark."

"Very well. I want him to be ready to start about eleven thirty, perhaps a quarter of an hour sooner than that."

"Yes, sir."

The servant bowed and left the room. The Black Star took paper out of a drawer, and a box of rubber stamps, and began composing a letter that was to cause the chief of police, the sheriff and Roger Verbeck much chagrin before morning.

> To those poor fools whom it most concerns:
> I was amused at the manner in which you guarded the little cottage so well. That fake headquarters was placed there in order to have you send all officers to the National Trust Building. I understand it fooled even Roger Verbeck. You

may place all the blame on the sheriff, since he responded so well to my decoy. While you guard the National Trust, I shall be looting the First National of the shipment of currency it received today. It is the first blow in my campaign. And when you learn that I am looting it, and rush there, I shall—But you will know what by the time you read this note.

The Black Star put the folded note into an envelope, and addressed it to the chief of police. Then he composed another to be mailed to a prominent newspaper.

I, the Black Star, begin my campaign tonight. Three nights from now, I and my men shall steal certain jewels and art objects that are famous. You may guess what they are, and where. Guard all jewels and objects of art in the city, if you wish, but that will not prevent us from getting them.

The Black Star put the letter into an envelope, addressed it, and then put both letters into one of his pockets. He glanced at his watch, and took off his robe, but retained the mask. He donned a heavy ulster, and rang for the servant again.

"Tell the mechanic to be ready in ten minutes," he said.

"Yes, sir."

"After I have left the house, throw on the protecting current, and do not turn it off unless you get the proper signal."

"I understand, sir."

"The wires were tested this afternoon?"

"Yes, sir; everything is in excellent condition."

"Good!" said the Black Star.

CHAPTER X

A DOUBLE CRIME

At a quarter of twelve that night, a man walked rapidly through the alley behind the First National Bank. He knocked on the basement door of the building adjoining. The door was opened by a watchman.

"Everything's all right," the watchman reported.

"Did you attend to that other fellow?"

"He'll sleep for a couple of hours yet."

"Fine work. You are to disappear after this, of course. Go to the hiding place arranged for you, and you will be sent ample funds. You are not to attempt to leave the city until you get orders to do so. Understand?"

"Sure. I know my business, all right."

"You'd better! The boss is going to be mighty strict during this campaign of his. The man who makes a mistake or disobeys orders won't last very long. Where are the robes?"

The watchman opened a box, took out a robe, and handed it over. The other man put it on quickly, affixed the mask, and started toward a door that opened into the basement of the bank building adjoining. At the door, he turned again.

"Let the others in, and tell them that they are to hurry," he told the watchman. "They'll give the usual signal, of course. Hand them their masks and gowns."

He opened the door and hurried into the other basement, went up a flight of steps, unlocked another door, and was on the first floor of the bank.

Down in the basement, the watchman admitted other men who arrived two minutes apart, until twelve in all were in the building, and gave them robes and masks. They hurried into the other basement and up the stairs, and took up their positions.

Some guarded the stairways that led to the second floor. Others were scattered around the first floor, watching the doors and windows. Two hurried into the vault room.

The shades had been drawn at all the windows, and were fastened securely at the sides and bottoms so that no light could be seen from the outside. An electric torch was flashed on the door of the vault, and held there, and one of the men began working on the lock with tools taken from beneath his robe.

"It's a cinch!" he whispered. "The more intricate they are, the easier it is to open them. I didn't work once in a safe factory for nothing!"

Save for the rasping of tools against steel and the heavy breathing of the man who worked, there was silence in the vault room and in the rest of the building. Presently there came a sharp click, the workman gasped his satisfaction and stood up. The big door was pulled open.

Both men hurried inside the vault. They began stuffing packages of bills into canvas bags which had been in the box with the robes.

"That's all!" one of them whispered to the other. "The boss said for us not to bother with securities or any of the small stuff. We'll go!"

"We'd better, or they'll be on us in another minute," the other man replied nervously. "When you opened that door you sent in an alarm."

"And it went to a protective agency where the man on night duty is one of us," the other replied, chuckling. "He'll have to give out the alarm, of course, but by the time he gives it out, we'll be far away. What time is it now?"

"Twelve thirty."

"Just right! Send the signal to the others. The lieutenant is standing by the window at the end of the hall."

A hiss escaped the man's lips, and was carried and echoed

through the building. The men gathered in the corridor, the lieutenant made sure all of them were there, and then they descended into the basement, and passed from it to the one adjoining.

"Signal for the autos," the watchman was ordered. "Then make your own get-away. And be sure you remember all that you've been told. Obey orders!"

The watchman stepped into the dark alley, and flashed an electric torch five times. A chauffeur at the mouth of the alley counted the flashes, and honked his horn. A procession of four automobiles started through the alley.

They did not stop, but merely slowed down, and into each machine sprang the men who had been assigned seats there. The automobiles continued through the alley and turned into the next street, where the chauffeurs put on speed.

There were few persons in that particular section of the city at the time, but those who were on the street saw the automobiles filled with robed and masked men. They knew what that meant—that the Black Star's band was working in the vicinity. Their terror kept them dumb until the automobiles had disappeared, and then they gave the alarm. They knew that there was but one thing in that section that would attract the master crook—and that was the vault of the old First National. The alarm went to police headquarters.

A few blocks down the street, the automobiles scattered, and one by one made their way to dark parts of the town, where the men in them took off their robes and masks, and, one by one, left the machines and darted away.

The band was scattered fifteen minutes after the vault had been looted, and one machine, a closed one, was running out along the river road toward the resort. The chauffeur drove in a leisurely manner, and the car attracted no undue attention.

At the end of the lane running to the old farmhouse, where it was pitch dark, the door of the closed car was opened, and a man sprang out. The automobile went on along the river road.

The man who had jumped from it carried two canvas bags stuffed with currency. He was Landers, the Black Star's trusted lieutenant.

Landers hurried along the lane, entered the grove about the house, and took a telephone from its hiding place behind a clump of brush. He called the house, and the servant who remained on guard at the headquarters answered.

Landers gave a password, then put the telephone away and sprang to his feet. He came to the wire fence that ran around the house, but he did not touch it. He knew that it was charged with a deadly current. A light flashed in a window, and Landers opened the gate and went on to the house. He disappeared inside. His work for the night was done, except that he had to turn in the swag.

But the Black Star and his band were not done for the night. The men who had left the automobiles and scattered, immediately made their way to the National Trust Company's building, and lost themselves in the throng of people there. They bumped elbows with policemen and deputies and detectives, and grinned when they recognized one another in the crowd.

They were in time to hear the alarm given, and to see policemen spring into automobiles and hurry away. They saw Muggs drive through the crowd, and Roger Verbeck spring into the roadster and start for the First National Bank. Word flashed through the crowd that the master rogue's band was looting the First National, and the crowd melted away like snow beneath a blazing sun, hurrying toward the scene of the robbery.

One by one, and cautiously, the Black Star's men entered the alley behind the National Trust Company's building. Here, too, a basement door was opened for them by a watchman. Once more they put on masks and gowns from a supply that was in readiness, and posted their guards in the building. Once more two selected men hurried into the vault room.

They began their work on the door of the vault; and suddenly the Black Star himself appeared before them, his face masked, the flaming star of jet on the hood of his robe.

"Make it as quick as possible!" he ordered. "We don't want to be here too long. Did things go all right at the other place? Was the get-away good?"

"Everything went off as planned, sir," one of the men reported. "The work was done to the minute, and the get-away was as you had ordered, sir."

"Disguise your voice when you speak to me, you fool!" the Black Star said. "And hurry with that vault! We can't spend all night getting inside that box!"

The rasping of tools against steel, the heavy breathing of the workman told that the man was doing his best to hurry. But the vault of the National Trust Company was a complicated affair, and it was a quarter of an hour before the door finally was swung open.

"Lively, now!" the Black Star commanded. "Those bags of gold are what we want—and all we want here at this time. Get them to the rear door as soon as possible, and signal for the autos. All you men get busy!"

The masked and robed members of the band carried the heavy bags from the vault, hurried through the corridor with them, went down the stairs, and to the basement door.

The Black Star watched the work. When it was completed, he walked across the room to the nearest telephone, took down the receiver, and gave the number of police headquarters.

"Is the chief there?" he asked.

"He's here, but he's busy. What do you want with him? Who is this?" the desk sergeant demanded.

"I think he'll talk to me, all right. This is the Black Star talking."

There was an exclamation at the other end of the wire, and

presently the chief spoke.

"Hello! This is the chief!"

"This is the Black Star! Did my new searchlight puzzle you a bit tonight, chief? When you know the secret you'll be more startled than puzzled. Did you wonder where my voice came from, and how I happened to be in the air just over you? Maybe you got the idea that I was putting on a ventriloquist's act."

"We'll get you, you fiend!" the chief cried angrily into the transmitter.

"Why, chief, how violent you sound! I am afraid you are working yourself into a passion."

"You got away with it this time, but you'll not do it again. And you had to lie to do it this time!"

"Indeed? How is that?"

"You used to boast of what you were going to do, and dare us to catch you at it, and you always told the truth in those days. You must be losing your nerve. You said, you crook, that you were going to rob the National Trust—and then you went after the First National."

"Oh, that was just a little job on the side!" the Black Star said. "I told you no falsehood, chief. I said that I would rob the National Trust, and that is exactly what I have done. I am speaking from the vault room of the National Trust this very minute. I have just removed several bags of gold coins!"

"What's that?" the chief cried.

"I am leaving a letter here in the vault room for you, chief, and have just mailed another to a certain newspaper. You'd better come right over here and get your letter, chief. And thanks so much for rushing all your silly policemen over to the First National when you got the alarm, so they would not bother my men here. It was very thoughtful of you!"

The Black Star laughed, and put up the receiver. He laid the letter addressed to the chief in the middle of the table, and pasted little black stars around the room on the marble. He ran to a rear window and saw three automobiles passing through the alley. In them were his men, he knew, and also the gold coin taken from the supposedly impregnable vault of the National Trust.

The Black Star laughed again, went to the stairs, and began mounting them, flight by flight, stopping now and then to laugh at a bound and gagged watchman. Presently he reached the roof by means of a trap door. He closed the door again, and fastened it securely. Then he took an electric torch from his pocket, and flashed a signal toward the sky.

He removed his robe, rolled it up, put it beneath his arm. He picked up his heavy ulster from the roof, where he had left it before descending into the bank, and put it on.

Once more he pointed the electric torch upward and flashed a signal. Then he touched match to cigarette, walked to the edge of the building, and glanced over.

He heard the sirens of police automobiles in the distance. He saw the machines stop and policemen spring from them. He watched as they gained entrance to the building, saw a crowd gathering in the street below. The Black Star chuckled again, took a vapor bomb from the pocket of his ulster, and hurled it at the street. It struck, exploded, and a cloud of white, pungent vapor drifted across the pavement. Shrieks and cries of alarm reached his ears. He saw one policeman stagger and fall, overcome by the gas.

The Black Star, still chuckling, walked back to the middle of the roof. He flashed another signal, and then returned the torch to his pocket.

He laughed again—and waited!

CHAPTER XI

MORE MYSTERY

Police headquarters was thrown into a turmoil for the second time that night when the chief received the master criminal's telephone message.

Roger Verbeck and Muggs rushed for the roadster, sprang in, and drove like mad through the streets toward the National Trust Company's building.

The chief shrieked his orders, officers tumbled into department automobiles, and followed Verbeck. They reached their destination, and sprang out. Verbeck already had ascertained that the front doors of the bank were locked and bolted. He rushed around to the alley, followed by Muggs, the chief, and a dozen officers. A detective hurried to telephone Sheriff Kowen.

The basement door was open, and they rushed inside. They found the watchman bound and gagged—he was a member of the Black Star's band, but they needed him again, and so made the attempt to remove all suspicion.

"The Black Star!" he gasped when they had removed the gag and bonds. "He was here with his gang! They carried out gold—went away in autos and—"

Verbeck had rushed on to the vault room. The chief and some of the others followed. They found the door of the vault standing open, money scattered on the floor, papers in confusion.

"He cleaned out all the big stuff!" the chief said. "One of you men telephone the president of the trust company and tell him to hurry down here."

"Here's the letter he mentioned, chief," Verbeck said.

The chief ripped it open and read it, then thrust it into one of his pockets. As he turned away, there was a sharp explosion in the street, then a bedlam of shrieks and cries. They rushed to a window and threw it open.

"Bomb!" somebody in the street was shouting. "It came from the roof!"

"One of that crook's gas bombs!" the chief exclaimed. "On the roof, is he?"

Verbeck already was running toward the stairs, with Muggs just behind him, determined to be in the midst of the affair. Muggs had been complaining again that he was not playing a principal part in this drama, and that he felt he was entitled to one.

Half a dozen officers took after them, the chief bellowed orders and posted guards throughout the bank. He sent other men to the floors above to release the watchmen. And then he followed Roger Verbeck, running up the stairs, puffing and panting, wishing that the elevator was running.

They came to the little steel stairs that led to the trapdoor and the roof. Verbeck tried to open the door, and found that it was fastened on the outside.

"Either the Black Star or some of his men are up there!" Verbeck said. "The door wouldn't be locked on the outside, otherwise."

One of the detectives had procured a fire ax from the hall on the floor below. He ran up the steel stairs and attacked the heavy door vigorously. The chief sent a man for another ax.

More officers had come up the stairs now, and stood at the bottom of the steel steps, waiting for the trapdoor to be opened.

"As soon as we get through, rush up there and go at them," the chief directed. "We don't know how many are up there, so be ready to mix it! Shoot, if you have to, but get him alive if you can. And look out for vapor guns and gas bombs!"

"Somebody on the roof is asking for you, chief!" the man

with the ax called down.

The chief hurried up the steps. "Well, who is it?" he demanded.

"This is the Black Star. Can't you recognize my voice? Still practicing violence, I see, and this time on a door!"

"Well, what do you want?" the chief cried. "Do you want to give yourself up?"

"Certainly not, my dear chief. I just wanted to let you know that I was here."

"And we're going to get you!" the chief cried. "If it is necessary we'll get you with a gun! If you start using that vapor stuff when we get the door open, my men will shoot. Understand that? I'll give you one minute to surrender and open the door!"

"Why on earth should I do such a thing as that?" the Black Star wanted to know.

"Because you are at the end of your rope, that's why!" the chief replied. "If you try to go down a fire escape, you'll be plugged. And that's the only way you can get off the roof."

"I have no intention of going down a fire escape," the Black Star replied. "I give you my word of honor—or dishonor, if you prefer it that way—that I shall descend no fire escape tonight. Does that satisfy you?"

"Are you going to give yourself up?"

"Dear me, no! I couldn't think of it. I have had a very pleasant evening, chief—very pleasant indeed—and profitable, also. By the way, did you get your letter?"

An exasperated chief descended the steps and motioned for the detective to go to work with the ax again. The heavy blows began raining against the door. Between them, they could hear the Black Star laughing.

"Get through that door!" the chief shrieked. "We've got him in a trap!"

"I wouldn't be too sure of that," said Roger Verbeck. "He

seemed to speak with confidence."

"But how can he get away?"

"The Black Star used to be noted for doing some peculiar and seemingly impossible things," Verbeck reminded the chief.

"I want to be the second man through that door!" Muggs said. "I got it comin' to me, boss. You ain't let me do a thing today, and I want to get my hands on that big crook!"

"That's what we all want to do," the chief remarked. "Get ready, men; that door will be open in a minute!"

The detective had succeeded in cutting a hole in it. Now he put his face close to the aperture and looked out. He could see nothing but darkness. Cautiously, he extended a hand and felt for the bolt, located it, shot it back. He whispered the news to those behind him. The officers crowded the steel stairs, and Muggs got well in the van. Muggs declined to be sidetracked longer.

The detective threw the door open, and they stumbled up the steps and to the roof, their weapons held ready, to dart to either side, expecting a shot, or a vapor bomb at least.

Their electric torches flashed, and the roof was bathed in light. There was nothing behind which a person could hide, except two chimneys. The officers approached the chimneys, carefully, ready for instant combat. They circled them—and found nobody.

"He's here—got to be here!" the chief cried.

They rushed to all the fire escapes and found that nobody was on them. They shouted to officers in the street below, and were told that the fire escapes had not been used. They searched every square foot of the roof, looked along the parapet, found nobody.

"I tell you that crook's got to be here!" the chief shouted. "How could he get away?"

"Airplane," one of the detectives suggested.

"Don't be an ass!" the chief shrieked. "An airplane makes a

lot of noise. And it wouldn't be easy to pick up a man from a roof in the dark, you fool! The only way it could be done would be to trail a rope and let him grab it, and that would mean a dead man on the pavement below. You ass, an airplane travels with speed!"

"Well, he doesn't seem to be here," Verbeck offered.

"But where could he have gone?" the chief cried. "Even the Black Star can't make himself invisible at will!"

Then they heard the Black Star laugh derisively.

They flashed their torches and again searched the roof. Once more they heard the laugh. Now it seemed to be to one side of them, and now to another. Above them, behind them, in front of them they heard it.

"This thing will drive me crazy!" the chief cried. "Flash those torches again! That crook is somewhere right here on the roof! Look for another trapdoor!"

They searched the roof, and found nothing; but again they heard the laugh, only it sounded far away now. Suddenly the roof was bathed in bright light that seemed to come out of the sky.

"He's up there—on something!" the chief shrieked.

They emptied their revolvers and automatics toward the sky. The light died out, flashed forth again and almost blinded them. Once more they heard the sarcastic laugh of the Black Star, as if far in the distance—and then the light was gone.

They stood silent, looking upward. Not the slightest sound came to their ears, except echoes of the shouts in the street below, where people were wondering about the peculiar, blinding light.

"What does it mean?" the chief cried. "Verbeck, what has that devil done?"

"I haven't the faintest idea," Roger Verbeck replied. "I don't understand that laugh, and I can't imagine where that light comes from. I'd think naturally, that it was an airplane, but, as you said, it would be almost impossible to pick a man off the roof at night—and an airplane makes a lot of noise. And we didn't hear a sound—remember that!"

Once more the voice of the Black Star reached their ears. He seemed to be shouting to them, and to be not so very far away.

"Good night, gentlemen!" he called to them. "It has been a splendid evening of amusement and profit. Good night—and let me express the hope that you'll have pleasant dreams!"

That was all. Though they waited on the roof for half an hour longer, they heard nothing more from him, saw nothing of him, and finally they turned and went back down the stairs, puzzled, angry, but determined to make the master rogue pay.

CHAPTER XII

ANOTHER TELEPHONE CALL

The newspapers the following day were full of the exploits of the Black Star. They explained that the master crook had inaugurated his campaign of crime and revenge by looting two of the richest financial institutions in the city. From the First National his men had obtained more than three hundred thousand dollars in currency. From the vault of the National Trust Company had been taken a quarter of a million in gold coin.

Banking officials were frantic. They made arrangements to safeguard their property, fearing to lose the confidence of their depositors. They engaged extra watchmen, men they knew personally, since to engage a stranger, no matter how good his references, might be to put one of the Black Star's men in the place.

Sheriff Kowen and his deputies were blamed, the chief and his policemen were declared incompetent and inefficient, and Roger Verbeck and Muggs were held up to ridicule.

The mysterious light that had come out of the sky was described at length, and many speculations made as to its nature. The scene on the roof of the building, told by one of the detectives, was played up, and there were many conjectures as to what it meant.

Had the master criminal come into possession of some wonderful new invention? Was he able to escape when and as he liked? Some inclined toward this belief, and others declared that the Black Star had gone down a fire escape under the noses of the officers, entered the building through a window at some floor, walked down the stairs and emerged into the alley and gone his way. The Black Star, one paper stated, was a mere man and did not call upon the supernatural to aid him. He merely had better brains than the police.

Where would he strike next?

Within three days, he had said in his letter to one of the papers, he would steal, with the aid of his band, jewels and famous objects of art. Thousands of persons had valuable jewels, and it was well known that the master criminal was a gem fiend, that he had a great collection and gloated over them. Perhaps he meant a jewelry establishment, a wholesale diamond house.

When it came to famous objects of art, there was a wealth of them in the city. Two millionaires had great collections. There was a famous museum that housed several hundred priceless paintings. Here and there throughout the city were others.

Jewels were carried to safe-deposit vaults. The guards at the museum were doubled. The two millionaires obtained police protection for their residences. And the city waited.

Two days passed, during which nothing was heard of the Black Star and his band. Sheriff Kowen and his deputies searched in vain for Mamie Blanchard. Roger Verbeck and Muggs drove about in the big roadster continually, watching people, trying to catch a glimpse of some known member of the Black Star's old organization.

The city was gone over, block by block, in an effort to locate the master crook's headquarters, but to no avail. The search extended to the suburbs, but nobody thought of the old farmhouse far up the river near the pleasure resort.

"Well, it's about time we heard from him again!" the chief said to Verbeck on the morning of the third day.

"I look for him to strike tonight," Verbeck said.

"And where do you think he'll strike?"

"That is the puzzle," Verbeck admitted. "I scarcely think he will attempt the museum. It would be a blow to civic pride if he did and succeeded, of course, but the odds would be against him."

"He seems to thrive on odds that are against him," the chief replied.

"Sooner or later, we'll get him!" Verbeck declared. "Sooner or later one of his people will make a slip that will give us the clew we need. They can't keep it up forever."

"But I want to land him right away!" the chief fumed. "Did you happen to read the morning paper? If this sort of thing keeps up, the mayor will be asking for my resignation, and I'll go out of office without having vindicated myself. Confound Kowen, anyway! Why couldn't he keep the crook when he had him? But for Kowen, the Black Star would be doing time in the big prison right now!"

"But he isn't—and it doesn't do any particular good to wail about it," said Verbeck. "The thing to do is to get him again. Made any plans?"

"I'm up in the air!" the chief complained. "What plans can I make? I've got men guarding the museum, and those millionaires' residences, and a few scattered near the jewelry establishments. And I'll hold men ready to go to any section of the city when we get an alarm. That is all I can do. If we knew where he was going to strike—"

A buzzer sounded, and the chief took up the telephone.

"Hello!" he called.

"That you, chief?"

"Yes."

"Ah, good morning. This is the Black Star! I have tapped a private line again, chief, to have a little chat with you! I've been resting for a couple of days, giving my men and women a holiday. But I'm eager to be busy again!"

"When I get my hands on you—" the chief began.

"Tut, tut! Why do you always grow violent when I do you the honor of calling you up?"

"Honor? Insult, you mean! We'll get you, and get you good,

one of these days!"

"I'll have all the wealth in town if you delay it very long," said the Black Star laughing. "By the way, chief, I'd suggest that you keep a lot of your men at headquarters tonight. You are going to need them."

"Think so?"

"I know it! And I have a faint idea that the newspapers are going to say more naughty things about you tomorrow. That was a pretty grilling the *Herald* gave you, wasn't it?"

"I'll give you a grilling when I get my hands on you!" the chief said. "So you're going to pull off some sort of a stunt tonight, are you?"

"I am. Inaction bores me, chief. My men are eager to get to work again. They take great pleasure in helping outwit the stupid men on your force."

"We'll see who'll do the final outwitting!" the chief cried. "I'm going to—"

"Going to get me, I think you said before. Sorry to dispute you, chief, but I can't agree. How do you expect to accomplish it?"

"Tell me one thing," said the chief. "How did you get off that roof, and where did you go?"

"Sorry, but that is a sort of state secret for the present," the Black Star replied.

"Well, if you didn't go down one of the fire escapes, write a letter to the newspapers and say so. They're swearing that you walked right out of that building before our noses."

"All right, chief, I'll inform the papers that I did nothing of the kind. But I'll not explain at this time just what I did do. You see, I might want to do it again soon."

"If you are so blamed sure of your ability, why not tell me what you are going to do tonight?"

"Gladly chief. I am going to collect some jewels and some

objects of art."

"Oh, are you?" asked the chief. "Going to collect them in any particular spot?"

"Naturally; but I do not intend to tell you the spot just now. That would be running too much of a risk, I am afraid. By the way, is Mr. Verbeck there?"

"He is!"

"I haven't time to speak to him, but will you kindly tell him for me that I hope he shows more speed in this little duel with me. I was disgusted with him the other evening—he showed no cleverness at all. Tell him that I hope he improves. And now, chief, I must end the conversation for the time being."

There was a click at the other end of the wire. The chief slammed the receiver into its hook and whirled around in his chair.

"Wanted me to tell you to show more cleverness and make the game more interesting, Verbeck," the chief said. "Make it interesting for him if we get the chance, all right! Says he's going to collect jewels and objects of art this evening."

"Then I suppose he'll do it," Verbeck said. "Have your men ready to jump out as soon as the alarm comes in. What is the sheriff doing, chief?"

"Kowen? Sleeping on the job, I suppose. He swears that he and his deputies will catch the Black Star—beat us to it. I had a row with him yesterday at luncheon. Kowen makes me tired! He's looking for that Blanchard woman."

"The Princess? He's not likely to find her," Verbeck said. "Either the Black Star has sent her out of the city, or she is in hiding some place where she'll not be located easily. You can wager that the Black Star takes good care of The Princess—she is one of the most valuable members of his band!"

CHAPTER XIII

INSIDE THE MUSEUM

That afternoon, about the hour of three, an elderly gentleman who looked like a person of culture and refinement, entered the Municipal Museum.

At the information desk, he asked concerning a certain painting, and was directed to the second floor. He thanked the woman at the desk and ascended the stairs, passing the close scrutiny of the guards and the police stationed there. There was nothing to cause suspicion in the appearance of an elderly man who evidently was a lover of art.

He found the painting for which he had asked, and stood before it for some time, looking at it, now stepping forward and now retreating, now and then walking to one side to get a better reflection of light on the canvas.

"Marvelous!" he said, in a thin voice, to one of the attendants. "Such coloring! And such technic!"

"Yes, them old boys knew how to sling the paint," the attendant informed him.

"Sling the paint? What a quaint idiom!" the elderly gentleman remarked and the attendant walked on, calling upon the world to witness that the crop of maniacs was getting larger every year, and that they all visited the museum.

Having inspected that particular picture to his evident satisfaction, the elderly gentleman went through the galleries, viewing other famous paintings. All the attendants and guides noticed him and put him down as a harmless art lover. There was a benevolent appearance about him; he appeared to be the sort of man who makes donations to museums and hospitals.

He finally made his way to the statuary hall. Here, at the

time, there was but one guide, and he was handling a group of four tourists. The elderly gentleman gave them scant attention. He adjusted his spectacles and began viewing the statue nearest the door, finished with that and went on to the next, and to the next. The guide and his tourists left the hall—and the elderly gentleman was alone there.

He walked quickly to the other end of the hall, turned and looked back at the door, and made sure that he was not observed by any of the attendants or visitors.

Above his head there was a small trapdoor that opened into the attic of the building. The elderly gentleman betrayed agility remarkable for his years.

He sprang to the nearest window ledge, sprang again and grasped the heavy molding, hung with one hand, and with the other pushed up the trapdoor. Then he pulled himself up and disappeared—and the door was put back in place.

The attic was seldom entered, it appeared. There was nothing at all stored there, and the dust was inches deep everywhere. The elderly gentleman made his way carefully through this dust, obliterating his tracks behind him, and reached a corner of the attic, near a window. Here was a dark space in a gable, large enough to accommodate a hiding man. The elderly gentleman sat down there.

"This will be the death of me!" he growled. "Dust and heat and foul air! I wish the Black Star had picked some one else for this part of the job!"

He took out a handkerchief and tucked it around the edge of his collar, then stretched himself between the rafters.

"Can't smoke—dare not sleep," he grunted. "And it'll be hours before I can get out of here. This is one sweet game I'm playing! But there'll be a handsome profit in it, all right!"

The hours passed. In the big museum below visitors came and went, passing beneath the scrutiny of the guards and the police. Five o'clock came, and the rooms were cleared. Guards searched them well, made sure nobody was inside the building except those who had a right to be there. The custodian and his assistants left. The big doors were locked. Night guards and policemen remained, walking through the rooms. Down in the basement an engineer threw a big electric switch that sent a powerful current through the frames that guarded the priceless objects of art.

Much had been made of that scheme of protection in the newspapers. When that current was turned on, any person touching one of the paintings would be rendered unconscious immediately. Moreover, an alarm would be sounded in the building, another flashed to police headquarters, another to the sheriff's office.

"The Black Star will never tackle this place," said one of the policemen to a guard. "He's going after something else. His gang couldn't get near the building without the men outside spotting them, and we could put up a scrap and keep them out until help came from headquarters."

"I think he'll tackle the private collection of some millionaire," replied the guard. "I don't see how he could hope to get in here and get away with anything."

Outside the building, police paced beats beneath bright lights that illuminated every door and window. Inside, more police and the regular museum guards talked and smoked and wished the long night was over.

Up in the attic, a perspiring elderly gentleman, who was elderly no longer because he had removed a very clever wig, and perspiration had ruined his make-up, looked at the radium dial of his watch and grunted that, at last, the time had come. It was nine o'clock.

He got up and made his way slowly and carefully across the attic through the dust to the trapdoor. He lifted it a fraction of an inch and looked down.

The statuary hall was dark save for a small incandescent light that glowed in the wall near the door. No guard or policeman was in sight, and the door leading to the corridor was closed.

The trapdoor was opened wide, and the man dropped to the floor, making not the slightest sound as he struck. He had removed his shoes in the attic, and had put on a pair of rubbers. He darted behind a statue, and listened, and wiped the perspiration from his face.

Then, running lightly from statue to statue, he made his way toward the corridor door, watching it continually, ready to dart into hiding if it should be opened by guard or policeman.

At the door, he stopped again to listen, and then he turned the knob and opened it cautiously. There was nobody in the corridor as far as he could see in either direction. The guards and policemen, it was evident, were on the floor below.

He took one of the Black Star's vapor guns from his pocket and held it ready. He slipped into the corridor, darted into a niche in the wall, listened again. He could hear two policemen talking on the floor below.

A guard entered the corridor and disappeared into one of the rooms. The man in the niche waited until he came out and started down the hall. The guard passed within three feet of him. The silent vapor gun was discharged, the guard gasped and started to cry out, but unconsciousness claimed him.

The man who had used the vapor gun drew the unconscious guard back into the niche. He used a hypodermic needle on the guard's arm, drugging him so that he would remain senseless for some time to come.

"No need to worry about you for a few hours," he growled.

Still he waited, going to another niche on the other side of the wide corridor. Another guard came from the floor below and started along the hall. He received the same treatment the first guard had received.

Then the man who held the vapor gun hurried through the

corridor and came to the head of the wide staircase.

"Ten men inside, and I've taken care of only two of them," he growled. "The boss certainly gave me my share of work to do in this little affair!"

He saw two policemen sitting at the bottom of the stairs. He saw a guard in the distance, another just emerging from one of the rooms on the floor below.

"Where are George and Fred?" he heard the guard ask.

"Went to the second floor," one of the policemen replied.

"Guess I'll go up and help them, and then we won't have to bother about the second floor until early in the morning. Get the card table ready, and we'll have a little game. Nothing to worry about. Looks to me as if the Black Star didn't intend to come here. I guess the boys on the outside would let us know if there was any danger."

The guard started up the stairs, and the man lurking at the top darted into the first niche and crouched there in the semi-darkness. The guard passed, the vapor gun was exploded, and the guard toppled forward as had the others, and was drugged as the others had been.

"Seven more, and the engineer," growled the Black Star's man.

Once more he went to the head of the stairs. Four policemen were putting out a collapsible card table. Two guards were approaching along the corridor. The seventh member of the protective squad, the Black Star's man knew, was at the front door, where the officers outside could see him. He was supposed to show himself there at the end of each hour, to let them know that everything was all right inside.

The Black Star's man darted through the corridor and went softly down the rear stairs. He made his way through the hall toward the front. He knew where the light switch was located; he had found this out several days before, when preparing for this night's events.

He reached the switch, jerked it down, and plunged the lower floor in darkness. He darted forward as he heard the exclamations of the six men in front. He dropped behind a statue just as one of the policemen flashed his electric torch.

"Fuse out, I suppose," he heard one of the guards say. "I'll get the engineer—he attends to all that stuff."

He hurried toward the basement entrance. The man at the front door merely shouted to know what was the matter, and remained at his post.

The five others were clustered about the card table. The Black Star's man crept forward and took a vapor bomb from beneath his coat. This was the perilous moment, he knew. This particular bomb was a delicate one that would make no noise as it exploded. But unless the vapor struck into the nostrils of the five men, disaster might come. If one of them escaped unconsciousness for a moment, he would be able to give the alarm.

Another bomb came from beneath the coat. The first one was hurled to the marble floor at the back of the five men. The second followed it.

Clouds of vapor arose. The Black Star's man held a sponge to his nostrils, flashed his torch and watched. It had worked—the five men were staggering—had fallen!

He had swift work to do now. At any moment the guard might return with the engineer, or the other guard come from the front door. He knelt beside the first man, and drove home the point of the needle. He worked in the dark, for it was safer that way. One by one he drugged them, and then he darted noiselessly toward the door that led to the basement.

He was just in time—the guard and engineer were coming up.

"Guess it's a fuse," the guard was saying. "Lights on the upper floor are still burning."

They stepped into the dark corridor, and the guard called for one of the policemen to flash his torch. The Black Star's man stepped up close, and again the vapor gun was discharged. They staggered and fell.

The needle was used again, and then he darted toward the entrance. The guard there had reported to the one outside, and was returning.

"Hurry up with those lights!" he shouted.

He gasped; collapsed. The Black Star's man caught him and let him down to the floor. He was holding the sponge to his nostrils again.

"I'll be going asleep from that vapor myself in a minute, if I'm not careful," he told himself. "I've hardly any more of the stuff. It's a good thing they're all down and out!"

He lifted the unconscious guard and carried him to one side, where he could not be seen from the entrance. Then he ran through the corridor and threw the light switch again, so that those outside would think everything was all right in the interior.

Then he ran to the basement door, hurried down the steps, went to a big electric switch on the wall, and threw that. The deadly protective current was shut off all over the building.

Up the stairs he dashed to the second floor. He hurried to a window on one side of the building, took an electric torch from his pocket and flashed it seven times.

The flashes were observed by a man in a window across the street.

CHAPTER XIV

MISSING MASTERPIECES

A half a dozen policemen were on guard outside the museum. They walked around the building continually, and communicated at the end of each hour with one of the guards inside. Now and then they gathered near the entrance to talk and wish their vigil was over.

Ten minutes after the Black Star's man had flashed his torch from the window, these six officers were startled by sounds of an altercation in the street. Two men, their voices raised, were quarreling. Others passing in the street stopped to listen. Threats were hurled back and forth. The men grappled, started to fight.

Two of the policemen left the museum and started running toward the combatants. When they were halfway one of the fighting men darted backward, drew a revolver and began firing.

There was a crowd on the corner now. The quarrelsome one continued to shoot; the other man fell in the street.

The four other policemen forgot the museum. They ran toward the corner, clubs in their hands, to beat back the crowd, to help take charge of the murderer, to send for an ambulance, if it proved to be necessary.

The Black Star's man observed this from a window. He flashed his torch again, and then ran down the stairs and to a little side door of the museum, which he unlocked.

Four men darted across the street and through this door. It was locked again immediately.

"All of them down and out!" the man who had been inside reported. "We'll have to work swiftly. They'll be expecting a guard to show his face at the door at the end of the hour. Come with me—I know the paintings the boss wants."

"How about that electric current?" one asked.

"I turned it off, of course. Hurry!"

They ran up the stairs and into one of the galleries. The man who had been inside indicated six paintings. Men crawled beneath the protecting railings, drew knives and started cutting the paintings from their frames.

"No time to waste!" the leader informed them. "We've got about fifteen minutes more."

He ran to one of the windows and glanced out at the street. The crowd was growing larger. The police had ascertained that the man who had fallen was not shot, but had stumbled in his mad haste to get away. The two men had been arrested, and the patrol auto called. None of the police had started back toward the museum, though some of them glanced in that direction now and then.

Inside, the paintings had been cut from their frames and made into rolls. The rolls were tied up with rope and then lashed together.

"Out you go!" said the man who had hidden inside.

They hurried down the stairs and to the little side door. The one ahead opened it and glanced out.

"Coast all clear!" he announced.

Two went first, carrying the roll of paintings with them. The others left one by one, darted across the street, and each went in a different direction. Those with the paintings had an automobile waiting; they jumped in and were driven rapidly away.

The men who had fought were carried away to jail; their part had been done well. The policemen went back to the museum, joking about the fight they had witnessed.

"They'll make it up in the morning and get fined for fighting and discharging firearms," one of them declared. "Business quarrel, eh? Pretty vigorous business men, I think!"

"Suppose everything's all right inside?" another asked.

"That gang inside is so busy playing cards that they wouldn't know it if a battle was staged in the street."

The end of the hour came, but no guard showed himself at the front door to say that everything was all right. One of the policemen pounded upon it, but got no response.

"That's funny!" he said. "They ought to answer—that's their orders!"

He pounded upon the door again, and still he got no reply from those inside.

"Think we'd better go in?" one of the others asked.

"We've got orders not to do it unless we know there's trouble inside."

"Well, there may be trouble."

"Card game—that's all. You listen to me—hand that guard a call down when he shows up. He's a sort of fresh guy, anyway—thinks he owns the museum, I guess!"

Once more he pounded on the door and got no response. The police began to look serious.

"Aw, how could anything happen?" one of them asked. "Nobody could get into the museum, could they? And there was nobody in there when it was locked up except them that belonged. Ain't we been on watch?"

"Well, that scrap called all of us across the street for a time, remember."

"Yes, and we'd better forget that if there happens to be any trouble inside. I think we'd better go in and investigate. This doesn't look exactly good to me."

He took a key from his pocket—a key to the front door of the museum, that had been given him for just such an emergency. He unlocked the door and went in with two of the others, locking the door behind him.

They hurried through the entrance and started down the

corridor toward the wide stairs that led to the floor above. The one in advance gave a cry of horror and started forward. Stretched on the marble floor were policemen and museum guards, unconscious, and plainly drugged in some manner.

"Call headquarters!" one of the policemen shrieked. "Get the chief!"

Another ran to the nearest telephone, which happened to be in the office of the custodian. Within a short time he had the chief on the wire.

"This is Officer Riley, at the museum," he said. "There's something wrong here. No guard showed up at the front door at the end of the hour, and so we came inside. We found all the guards and officers unconscious, laid out!"

"What's that?" the chief cried. "What laid 'em out? What's happened out there?"

"We just got inside the building—haven't had time to investigate—don't know what's been going on!" Officer Riley gasped. "Thought I'd better call you at once."

"Keep your eyes open—we'll be right up there!" the chief cried. "Keep right on the job!"

"Better bring the police surgeon with you, chief. There seems to be something wrong with these men."

That telephone conversation caused another tumult at police headquarters. The chief bellowed his orders, then ran with Verbeck and Muggs to the former's roadster, which was in readiness at the curb. With Verbeck at the wheel, the powerful car dashed through the streets toward the museum, and behind it came half a dozen police department autos filled with detectives.

They reached the museum, left the cars and hurried to the entrance. One of the men inside unlocked and opened the door.

"They are still unconscious, chief!" he reported. "Looks to

me as if they had been doped."

The police surgeon made a swift examination.

"They have been drugged," he announced, "and pretty badly, at that. I'll have to get busy on them at once, or we'll have dead men on our hands."

"Bring them around as soon as you can," the chief said. "I want to hear what they've got to say. And you men search the entire building! We'll look into this! One of you call up the superintendent of the museum and get him down here. Lively!"

The officers scattered throughout the big building, turned on all the lights, and began their search. They found the unconscious guards on the upper floor and carried them below for the police surgeon to work on. The surgeon sent in a call for his assistants.

Policemen who searched the statuary hall discovered the open trapdoor. They got up into the attic, and investigated there, and found nothing except dust and footprints in it. Down to the first floor they went to report this.

Verbeck and Muggs hurried to the attic and investigated for themselves.

"Very simple," Verbeck said. "Some member or members of the gang got up here during the day, remained in hiding until night, and then got down and handled the guards and officers."

"Yeah, but where are they now?" Muggs wanted to know.

"Not in the building, you may be sure. They managed to get out in some manner."

"And what did they swipe?"

"The superintendent will have to tell that, I suppose. There are several thousand things in this place, Muggs, that are almost priceless. The Black Star has done it again. Let's go downstairs and see if there is anything in the nature of a clew."

They hurried down the stairs. The superintendent of the museum had just arrived—a worried, frantic superintendent who immediately telephoned for more guards and one of his assistants.

"I am almost afraid to look," he announced. "Do you suppose anything has been taken?"

"That little side door is unlocked," one of the detectives reported to the chief.

"It shouldn't be," said the superintendent. "It always is locked except when we are receiving new exhibits, which are delivered at that entrance."

Verbeck grasped one of the officers by the arm.

"Have you watched closely all night?" he demanded.

"Yes, sir."

"Didn't leave the museum at all?"

"For a few minutes. There was a shooting scrape at the corner—"

"Did all of you go there? How long were you gone? Speak quickly, man!"

"Weren't gone more than half an hour. But we watched the museum, just the same. It's light—"

"From the corner you couldn't see that little side door!" Verbeck thundered. "Any of the Black Star's men who had hidden in the museum could have rendered these guards and officers unconscious, taken what they wished, and walked right out of that side door with it, while you were over at the corner. That fight was staged for a certain purpose!"

"Oh, you fools!" the chief cried. "The newspapers are right— the police force is a gang of imbeciles! Idiots! You've let him get away with it again!"

The superintendent of the museum had been going through the building with a couple of detectives, and now they heard his cry of surprise and rage from the upper floor.

"What is it? Find something missing?" the chief cried.

"Six famous paintings!" the superintendent shrieked. "Six of them gone! Six priceless masterpieces—cut from their frames—carried away! The protective current—it must have been turned off! Six of the most priceless pictures!"

"Great Scott!" the chief ejaculated.

"Now there will be a fine row!" Verbeck said. "We've got to catch the Black Star and get those paintings back! Every art lover will howl until we do! And, worst of all, they didn't belong to the museum—they were merely loaned. And the six are worth more than a million dollars!"

CHAPTER XV

SOME FISHERMEN

At his headquarters, the Black Star was pacing the floor nervously, his hands clasped behind his back. A buzzer sounded, and he hurried to the telephone, taking it from its hiding place in the niche in the wall.

"Hello!" he said.

"Number Eleven."

"Countersign?"

"Kokomo."

"Report," ordered the master crook.

"Everything went off as planned, sir. I got into the attic without much trouble, and subdued the guards and policemen when the proper time came. The fight was started as soon as the men received my signal."

"How about the loot?"

"We got all six of the paintings, sir, and they are on their way to you now."

"Good! That is all for tonight. Report at the usual time in person tomorrow."

The Black Star hung up the receiver, rang the bell three times, took the receiver down again. The ring was heard by men at a telephone instrument in the woods a quarter of a mile away.

"Hello!" one of them answered.

"Start!" the Black Star said; and then he hung up the receiver again and touched the bell button. The servant came into the headquarters room.

"Tell the mechanic to be ready to start within five minutes," the master rogue ordered.

The servant hurried away, and the Black Star took off his

robe and put on the heavy ulster once more. Presently he hurried from the room, closing and locking the door behind him.

In the woods, six men left the hidden telephone and hurried along a narrow, winding path through the darkness, going toward the bank of the river.

They did not speak as they hurried forward, single file, like Indians following a trail. They reached the shore, and in a little cove came upon a motor boat hidden beneath overhanging willows. The six got into the boat.

They moved the craft out into the stream and pointed its bow toward the city. The six were dressed as fishermen, in uncouth clothing, stubbles of beard upon their faces, their sleeves rolled up. In the launch was fishing gear. There was nothing in the appearance of the craft to create suspicion, but a mechanic, had he looked at the engine, would have marveled that common fishermen could possess such a perfect piece of machinery.

The regulation lights were burning. The launch made ordinary speed down the stream. Two of the men were singing raucously. To all appearances here were six fishermen going to the city to carouse at some cheap resort on the waterfront.

At the lower end of town, the launch turned toward the shore. At a small dock she was moored. But only five of the men left the boat—one remained curled up in the stern, hidden by a mass of canvas and fishing gear.

The five entered a cheap resort and drank, and then went upon the street again, as if starting to another place. They slipped through a dark alley, emerged on a side street and hurried along it, maintaining a conversation that had to do with fish and market prices.

After a time they came to a public square in an old section of the city. Here were business houses that had been there for scores of years, famous establishments that scorned to move to a more modern district of the town.

They stopped on a corner and talked loudly, half quarreling, as intoxicated fishermen might be expected to do. A policeman warned them to lower their voices and behave, and they went on up the street, slowly, staggering a bit, laughing now and then.

On the next corner was a bakery. The basement door was open, and a baker stood in it. Odors of fresh bread and cakes poured out.

"Um!" one of the fishermen gasped. "Any chance to get some hot bread?"

"Do you happen to have the price?" the baker asked.

"We sure have!"

A passing pedestrian heard the conversation, smiled, and walked on.

"Come downstairs, then," the baker said.

They descended the stairs and entered the oven department. They threw coins on a table, and each was given a loaf of warm bread, and they began eating, still laughing and talking. The baker's assistant had finished his work and washed up, and now was telling his employer good night. He hurried up the steps and went away.

The baker led the five fishermen into a rear room to show them more ovens, where cakes were baking. He closed the door between the two rooms. Instantly the demeanor of the five men changed.

"Everything all right?" one of them asked.

"There is one guard in the diamond room. The others are on the two floors," the baker replied.

"How many in all?"

"Only four."

"Cinch!" said one of the five. "Let's go!"

"I'll have the other stuff ready," the baker informed them.

He opened the door and glanced into the other room, closed the door again and motioned that everything was all right. The five men hurried to the other end of the room, and one of them pressed against the wall. A small door swung open.

They passed through the wall and into the basement of the building adjoining. An engineer was asleep in a chair before his table, and he was rendered unconscious immediately by means of a vapor gun. The five hurried up a flight of stairs, opened a door, and entered a rear hall.

They were at the back of a famous jewelry establishment now, one that had a famous name in the business world, one which scorned to move to better quarters, but which was protected by every known device. Another door was opened, and they were in a storeroom.

They moved with more caution now, for this was dangerous ground. The Black Star had planned this attack on the assumption that he would be expected to rob a more pretentious establishment. Few men knew that a large shipment of gorgeous diamonds had recently been received by this firm—but the Black Star knew it. One of his band was a trusted clerk in the house.

Moreover, at that moment, the Black Star was creating a diversion. In the principal retail district of the city there was a fashionable jewelry store housed in a modern building. It was being heavily guarded this night, for the proprietors had taken cognizance of the master crook's announcement that he intended to purloin rare jewels, and they flattered themselves that their establishment would be the one visited.

More than a score of special watchmen and police officers were in this building. One of the proprietors himself was on hand, aiding in safe-guarding the jewels. The entire establishment was brilliantly lighted. The shades and fire curtains at the windows were raised, and the door of the vault room stood open so that it could be seen from the front street. The Pioneer Diamond Company was taking no chances of being looted.

And suddenly the building that housed the diamond company was bathed in brilliant light that seemed to come out of the sky!

People in the streets, remembering what had happened three nights before, began shrieking that the Black Star and his men were at work. An alarm was sent to police headquarters, and relayed to the chief at the museum. The Black Star was robbing the Pioneer Diamond Company!

Leaving a small police guard at the museum, the chief hurried to the scene with the remainder of his men. Verbeck and Muggs went ahead in the roadster, charging through the streets, the horn shrieking a warning. As they arrived, the bright light had disappeared, but soon they saw it again.

"That's the Black Star," Verbeck said. "I can't figure out how he does it, but I suppose the solution will be simple enough when we learn it."

"I'd like to beat it out of him!" Muggs said.

The police had entered the building, and the chief had ascertained that nothing had happened. As far as they knew, there was nobody in the establishment who did not have a right to be there. But that did not mean that the danger was over.

"I don't like the looks of this!" Verbeck said. "I am inclined to believe that the gang is doing the real work in some other place."

"I've got men every place where there is any quantity of precious stones," the chief said, "and they have orders to send an alarm to headquarters the instant they see or hear anything that seems to be suspicious."

The bright light from the sky had disappeared again. Out in the street there was a series of explosions, and Verbeck and Muggs and the chief rushed to a window, and saw clouds of vapor rising from the pavement.

"He's got some scheme!" the chief declared. "Watch yourselves, you men, and be ready to go into action! More of you go into the vault room and watch there!"

The proprietor was like a maniac, and the chief whirled upon him angrily.

"What's the matter with you?" he demanded. "You don't see any of the crook's gang around here, do you? How can we do anything until they show up? You give me a pain."

"There is a fortune in the vault—"

"And it'll probably remain there!" the chief said. "We are playing a game that is tough enough without having an insane man raving around us!"

Another shower of vapor bombs came from the sky. The people in the streets were scattering, seeking cover. Once more the bright light blazed forth. Out into the street rushed Verbeck and Muggs. The light disappeared, and presently they heard the voice of the Black Star.

"Better watch those diamonds, gentlemen!" he shouted. "You'll be missing a lot of them the first thing you know. I love gems, and I happen to know that there are some glorious ones in the vault of the Pioneer Diamond Company."

The voice died away, and they heard no more. Verbeck and Muggs rushed back into the store. The chief was in the vault room.

"Are all your diamonds and expensive jewels in that vault?" the chief asked the member of the firm who was spending the night in the store.

"All except a few small stones such as the Black Star would not bother about."

"Then Mr. Black Star is going to fall down on the job!" the chief declared. "We'll just pack this vault room full of officers. The only way those crooks can get in then will be to tunnel through the bottom of the vault!"

"They can't do that—the vault is impregnable!" the member of the firm declared.

The chief laughed scornfully. "It may be impregnable as far as ordinary criminals are concerned," he retorted, "but we are dealing with the Black Star, please remember, and he dotes on supposedly impregnable things. Vaults do not seem to bother his men much. Open the door of the vault, and sit in it yourself. We'll watch the inside as well as the outside."

The door of the vault was opened. An investigation showed that everything was all right. And so they waited for the blow that they expected.

A telephone bell rang, and the member of the firm hurried to the instrument to answer.

"It's a call for you, chief, from your headquarters," he reported.

The chief rushed to the telephone. He was experiencing a feeling of apprehension.

"Hello!" he cried.

A desk sergeant at headquarters answered him.

"That you, chief? The Black Star's men are raiding a diamond store downtown. I just got the tip from a watchmen who dodged them. Wait—I'll give you the address!"

CHAPTER XVI

HOT BREAD

Far downtown, the five fishermen passed through the store-room and entered another hall. They walked through this to the end, making not the slightest noise. Each man held a vapor gun in his hand and was prepared to use it if occasion demanded.

At the end of the hall, another door was opened with a duplicate key one of the men took from his pocket. The five crept through, and closed the door again.

"Two men on each floor, and one in the diamond room," the leader whispered. "Make sure that we get them all."

The band scattered. Two remained on the lower floor, two started to the floor above, and one made his way toward the diamond room in the rear. Dim lights were burning here and there, and the men moved from shadow to shadow, noiselessly alert.

On the lower floor, the two watchmen were eating their night luncheon. They sat close together, talking in low tones. A light was burning above the table upon which they had put their lunch boxes, but the spot could not be seen from the street through the windows.

The Black Star's two men advanced carefully. One of them made a sign, transferred the vapor gun to his left hand, and took a bomb out of his pocket. He hurled it behind the two watchmen.

They sprang to their feet, gasped, dropped. The two members of the Black Star's band turned away and darted to the foot of the stairs, ready to help their companions if help should be needed.

On the second floor, the two watchmen were found separated and rendered unconscious immediately. The man who had gone toward the diamond room stopped just outside the door and peered in. The watchman inside evidently feared no interruption. He was sitting with his back to the open door, reading a newspaper.

A shot from the vapor pistol, and he was unconscious. Three of the other four men hurried into the room. The other remained below, on guard at the end of the hall through which they had entered.

Tools were taken from pockets, and work began on the door of the vault. Two of the band were experienced workmen in whom the Black Star took pride. They worked swiftly, yet thoroughly. They knew that opening the vault would take some time.

On the lower floor the two watchmen remained stretched on the carpet. Presently, one of them opened his eyes, then raised his head and looked around carefully.

It happened that he had inhaled very little of the vapor from the bomb. As he fell he had tottered to one side, and the draft from the nearest ventilator had carried the fumes away from him. He was a man who had read all the newspapers ever had printed concerning the Black Star's methods, and he guessed immediately what had occurred.

He did not know with how many men he had to contend. He supposed they were raiding the diamond room, and that there were guards posted, but could not be sure. He listened intently, glanced around again. He saw nobody, heard nothing except a slight sound that came from the diamond room, the rasping of tools against steel.

The watchman had been long in the service of the firm, and was a trusted man. But he also was an old man, and not very strong. He was not the sort to combat the Black Star's band single-handed, though he had a revolver in his pocket.

But he was the sort who would take a chance to give an alarm. He glanced at his unconscious companion, looked around the room again, and started crawling slowly over the floor, a foot at a time.

He came to the first aisle, and looked down it. There was nobody in sight. He crept along the counters, behind them, stopping now and then to listen. He was not making fast progress, but he was afraid to risk everything in the interests of speed.

Finally he reached the end of the counter, and once more he looked around and listened. He could still hear the slight noise in the diamond room, but that was all. He had an open space of twenty feet to cross now, and he proceeded faster, and finally reached the door of a private office.

He raised himself, opened the door noiselessly and entered. Then he sprang to his feet, locked the door, and darted to the telephone on the desk.

He had expected to find the telephone useless, and was gratified that such was not the case. Once more he paused to listen, and then lifted the receiver from the hook, and put his lips close to the transmitter.

"Number?" asked the girl at central.

"Police headquarters—quick!"

It seemed to him that he waited an eternity before the voice of the desk sergeant came to him over the wire.

"Robbery!" he gasped. "Black Star's men!"

"Where, man—where?" demanded the sergeant.

The watchman gave the address.

"This is one of the watchmen," he added. "The gas bomb didn't put me out, and I managed to crawl to the office. Hurry—hurry! They are in the diamond room now—I don't know how many of them! But hurry!"

Then the old watchman sank into the chair before the desk, weak and trembling. He had done his part, and he could not do more. He took out his revolver, and tried to decide whether he should attack them. It would be better, he thought, to wait until the police came—they would not be long.

Up in the diamond room the Black Star's men had opened

the vault door, finally. They reached for three certain trays, and swept the diamonds from them. They had orders what to get and what to leave—the master rogue wanted only some stones recently received, one hundred superior stones upon which a high valuation had been placed by experts.

With the gems in their pockets, they left the diamond room and closed the door behind them. They started down the hall to meet the men who had remained on guard.

And suddenly they heard police sirens shrieking, and the front of the establishment was bathed in light.

"The cops are on us!" one of them gasped.

"We needn't worry if we can get through the basement wall and into the bakeshop. But we'll have to hurry," another replied, rushing along the hall.

They darted down the stairs, closing and locking all the doors as they went, for they did not want the police to guess the manner of their entrance. The Black Star might have need of the baker in some other enterprise.

They came to the wall and tapped upon it. The baker swung the little door open, and they stepped into the shop.

"Cops all around the place!" he reported. "Must have been tipped off in some way. Where are the stones?"

"Here!" one replied, and tumbled them on the table.

Before the baker was a pan of dough. He worked swiftly, forming it into light biscuits—and into each biscuit he put diamonds. He put the biscuits into a pan, greased the tops of them, put the pan into one of the ovens.

"Two bottles of beer there—open them!" he ordered in a whisper.

One of the five fishermen obeyed. They poured the liquor out, drank a part of it, put their glasses down upon the table.

There was bedlam in the streets now. The police had surrounded the block. They were battering at doors, and the old watchman was letting them in at the front entrance. A crowd already had started to gather.

"Tight hole!" one of the fishermen said.

"Not unless you lose your nerve!" the baker answered. "Beginning to get scared?"

"I guess I've got as much nerve as the next man!"

"Then show it!" the baker said. "Make a wrong plan, and all of us will be in trouble. They are sure to come in here in a minute or two."

Verbeck and Muggs had entered the establishment with the chief. The old watchman told his story in a few words. Lights were turned on, and the place searched, and the unconscious men found. Then Verbeck hurried to the diamond room, with the others at his heels.

The door of the vault was open. Empty trays were on the floor; and at the bottom of the vault was a sheet of white paper, upon which had been pasted a row of little black stars.

"Looted!" the chief gasped. "But where can they be?"

"Gone before we got here!" Muggs said.

"The watchman says he heard them just as we came up. There are only two exits to the ground floor—the front door and the rear one—and no windows in the back large enough to permit a man to pass through."

"And the back door is bolted on the inside—I investigated it," Verbeck said.

"Then, where have they gone?" the chief cried. "This thing is getting on my nerves! But we've got the block surrounded, and every man inside the lines will give an account of himself."

The search of the block began, and it was a methodical and thorough one. Building by building, room by room it went on, while the crowds gathered outside. The chief took up his station on a corner and received reports that were highly discouraging. It appeared that the master criminal's men had disappeared into thin air, or else had left the place before the police arrived.

Verbeck and Muggs conducted an investigation of their own,

but found nothing to help them.

"This gets my goat, boss!" Muggs said. "I think it's a hoodoo to work with the cops."

"I'm beginning to think that myself, Muggs," Verbeck replied. "The Black Star tricks the police, and when we are with them we get tricked, too. Beginning with tomorrow, Muggs, you and I tackle the job on an independent basis."

"That's great, boss! And we'll get that big crook, too!"

"We'll get him!" Verbeck promised.

"And when we do, you turn your back for about five minutes, and let me handle him," Muggs begged. "I want to give him the sore throat, and give it to him bad!"

"Maybe you'll get the chance," Verbeck said.

Down in the bakeshop the five fishermen were making merry around the table. Upon them entered half a dozen policemen, a captain at their head.

"Who are you, and what are you doing here?" the officer demanded, looking at them suspiciously.

The five fishermen showed alarm in their faces. The baker rushed forward.

"Why, they're friends of mine, captain," he said. "They're fishermen, and come up from the wharf now and then at night to have a little drink of beer with me. I've known them for years."

"What are your names, and where do you live and work?" the captain asked.

They were ready with that information. They had prepared it in advance; and, if their answers were investigated, they would stand the test.

"Well, maybe you're all right, but we can't afford to take any chances," the captain said. "The Black Star's gang has made a haul in the jewelry house on the other side of the block, and we're taking a good look at every man around here. You'll have to stand a search, or be taken in!"

The five fishermen announced that they were willing to be

searched. The search was carried out immediately. From their pockets were taken knives, bits of twine, chewing tobacco, soiled handkerchiefs—things one would expect to find in the pockets of such men. They had, of course, hidden their vapor guns and their drilling tools in a safe place under the cellar flagstones before the police came upon them.

"Well, what are you hanging around here tonight for?" the captain demanded.

"They just came up to have a little drink with me, and to get some fresh bread," the baker explained. "They are waiting for it now—fresh-bread and light biscuits. Jim, there, is a fiend for my light biscuits."

As he finished speaking, the baker turned to his oven and opened the door. A delicious aroma streamed forth, and the men sniffed. Bread and biscuits were tumbled out, and the baker started wrapping them up.

"What did that gang get in the jewelry store?" he asked the captain.

"Don't know exactly—diamonds, I suppose. You men get your stuff and get out of here. I guess you're all right. How are you going to get home?"

"We've got a launch down at the wharf," one of them replied. "She ain't much to look at, and ain't any race horse, but she does manage to get through the water a bit. Good enough for our business, I reckon."

"Get your stuff and come along. I'll see you through the lines," the captain told them. "We'll have to search your shop, baker. I'll leave a couple of men to do that."

"All right. But I ain't in the diamond business," the baker said, grinning.

The captain opened the door and motioned for the five fishermen to pass him. He conducted them to the street and across it, and passed them through the lines. They went on toward the waterfront, talking loudly, swaggering and staggering a bit, jesting, and now and then singing a snatch of song.

Four of them carried a loaf of bread each. The fifth man carried a dozen light biscuits beneath his arm.

And in those biscuits was a fortune in diamonds!

CHAPTER XVII

MUGGS SEES HIS MAN

Again the morning newspapers carried full-page stories of the depredations of the Black Star and his band. Once more the police were called idiots, and demands were made that the chief resign. Sheriff Kowen was held up to scorn.

The newspapers carried another story, too—that Roger Verbeck had had a quarrel with the chief of police over the way the fight against the Black Star was being conducted, had left police headquarters with Muggs, too angry to speak to the reporters, and had declared afterward, when seen at his apartment, that he was done. Why should he perform the duties of the police and at the same time submit to the abuse of the imbecile chief, he was said to have asked? As far as he was concerned, the Black Star could loot banks and private residences and conduct himself as he pleased. Roger Verbeck might, within a few days, take himself out of the city and remain until there was some resemblance of law and order again.

The chief of police merely admitted that there had been trouble between himself and Verbeck, and said that he felt the police force capable of attending to its own affairs without any help from plain citizens, a remark that caused more than one caustic editorial.

The Black Star had sent another letter to the newspapers, and it made interesting reading. It was as follows:

To the Public:
  I said I would purloin famous objects of art and valuable jewels, and I have kept my word, as I always do. Some day when I have time, and it will not imperil any of my people to

do so, I shall send a letter telling just how it was done.

My campaign against the city has been highly successful so far, and I have no reason to believe it ever will be otherwise. The antics of the police and the sheriff and his deputies are particularly amusing to me; it would be more amusing if they were foemen worthy of my steel.

I shall rest for a day, and two nights from now shall resume my campaign. For the trouble I experienced during my incarceration, the city must pay in full. I do not even care to state the nature of my next exploit, but I guarantee that it will be sensational.

* * * *

Roger Verbeck and Muggs slept until noon that day, then had breakfast and read the newspapers. Verbeck's face glowed when he read of the quarrel between the police and himself.

"It may work, Muggs, and it may not," he said. "I fixed it up with the chief, and he certainly has done his part. The Black Star will have us watched for a few days, anyway, so we must be on our guard. But if he gets the idea that we are after him no longer, we may be able to pick up the trail."

"It's a hoodoo to work with cops!" Muggs declared. He had small respect for the police, a state of mind that was a relic of the old days when he had fought against them himself.

"Well, we'll see what we can do by working alone, Muggs. Have you anything to suggest?"

"Only that we find his headquarters, catch the crook in 'em, and give him all that's comin' to him!" Muggs said.

"That happens to be a large order, Muggs. If we can do those things, victory will perch on our banner."

"I didn't know Victory was a bird," said Muggs. "In pictures they always make her a woman."

"Muggs, that was a figure of speech—merely a manner of talking. Victory always perches on a banner, Muggs—don't forget it. I've read it a thousand times. Anything more to suggest?"

"You'd better go and see your girl," Muggs told him. "You ain't been to see her for almost a week, and she'll be gettin' peeved at you."

"I thought you hated the idea of me getting married."

"I do, but it can't be helped," Muggs retorted. "And she's some girl, at that. Besides, boss, if I drive you over there, and around town a bit, it is just possible that we might spot somebody who belonged to that crook's old gang."

"That's what I've been trying to do since he escaped, Muggs, and haven't had any luck," Verbeck said. "Get out the roadster."

"Roadster?"

"Yes; we shall not take Miss Wendell out with us. I'll visit her for a short time, and then we'll drive around town."

Muggs got out the car, and ten minutes later was driving Roger Verbeck across the city to the apartment house that was the home of Faustina Wendell, Verbeck's fiancée. Verbeck watched the people on the streets as they rode along, and Muggs did when it was possible, but they failed to see anybody for whom they were looking.

Verbeck hurried inside when the apartment house was reached, and Muggs crouched down behind the wheel, pulled his cap low over his eyes, and pretended to be half asleep. But he was scrutinizing every man and woman who passed the roadster.

Muggs was rejoicing secretly because Verbeck had elected to work independently of the police. That meant that Muggs would play a more active part in the affair, and he was as eager for a large part as an actor in a stock company. Muggs craved adventure and excitement, and the lust of combat was strong within him.

"I'd like to find the big crook!" he growled, as he watched the passers-by. "I'd like to find him with just the boss, and hand him a few and lug him off to jail and throw him in! Make fun of my boss in the newspapers, will he? The big stiff!"

Muggs glanced toward the apartment house. He supposed that Verbeck would remain there about two hours instead of a few minutes, as he did generally.

"I can't understand this love stuff!" Muggs said. "There's plenty of chances to fight without gettin' married. I suppose I'll have to keep dressed up all the time and stand in a corner after the boss gets back from his honeymoon. It's enough to make a man turn bad again! It's enough to—"

Muggs suddenly ceased speculating on marriage and the status of a valet in a family. He had spotted a man walking along the street, on the opposite side. He turned his eyes and watched him, and his heart almost stood still.

"Landers!" he gasped. "The Black Star's lieutenant—or anyway he was before. He's done somethin' to his face and hair, and he's fatter—but he's Landers. He's got a nerve paradin' the streets this way!"

This was something that Verbeck should know! But Roger Verbeck was visiting Miss Wendell, and she lived on the tenth floor, and in a rear apartment, with her mother. It would take Muggs several minutes to get inside the house and telephone up, and Verbeck several minutes to get down to the roadster. And Landers was signaling a taxicab!

Muggs darted inside the house and up to the desk.

"I'm Mr. Verbeck's chauffeur!" he said. "He's visitin' Miss Wendell. You phone up that Muggs had to hurry away—that he saw a man. He'll understand!"

Then Muggs dashed out to the street again, sprang into the roadster, started the engine, whirled the big machine around, and pursued the taxicab.

"This is tough luck!" Muggs told himself. "It's a cinch that Landers knows this car. He'll spot it in a minute, if we get out of the heavy traffic! I wish I had the boss along!"

The taxicab did not make good speed through the traffic, and

Muggs remained about a third of a block behind it. After a time it turned into a cross street, and presently stopped before an exclusive hotel. Muggs swung the roadster to the curb. He saw Landers get out, pay the chauffeur, and disappear into the hotel.

Muggs was out of the car instantly, and hurrying forward. He approached the entrance, and glanced in. Landers had not stopped at the desk, but had gone directly to an elevator. That meant that he was a guest, or a frequent visitor.

When the elevator came down again, Muggs hurried over and spoke to the boy.

"The gent that just rode up with you—" he began.

"Mr. Smith?"

"Maybe his name's Smith—I don't know. I just wanted to find out where he went—got a message for him—phoned it from the office over there."

"He comes here to visit Miss Whaley and her elder sister," the boy explained. "You just ring up No. 256, and I guess you can get him."

Muggs went across the lobby and into a telephone booth. But he did not call room 256. He called Verbeck at Miss Wendell's apartment, and got him on the wire.

"I spotted Landers, boss!" he said. "I trailed him to the New Nortonia Hotel. He calls himself Smith here, and he visits a couple of women who call themselves Whaley; they're in room 256."

"Great!" Verbeck cried. "Stay there until I come over, Muggs; I'll start right away."

"Suppose he leaves before you get here, boss?"

"Then trail him, Muggs, and telephone to me as soon as you can. I'll go back home if I miss you!"

Muggs went out on the street again and got into the roadster. He moved the car a bit nearer the hotel, and then thought better of it and circled to the other side of the street. And there he remained, watching the entrance of the hotel.

CHAPTER XVIII

MUGGS MEETS DISASTER

Muggs knew that it would take his master some time to get there from the apartment house, and he hoped that Landers would remain in the hotel until Verbeck arrived. Muggs began speculating, too, as to the identity of the two Misses Whaley. Probably they were members of the Black Star's organization.

Muggs was doomed to disappointment. Before ten minutes had passed, he saw Landers come from the hotel and start walking up the street. Muggs wheeled the roadster, and followed slowly. Landers was on the opposite side.

"I hope he don't look this way and spot me!" Muggs growled. "He sure would remember this car. There ain't another like it in town, and he saw plenty of it when we were after the big crook before. I sure hope he don't look this way!"

It appeared that Muggs was to have his wish. Landers walked briskly down the street for three blocks, and then stepped to the curb. A big touring car was standing there, and Landers spoke to the chauffeur and sprang in. The car started down the avenue, and Muggs followed in the roadster.

The touring car cut across the city, following the boulevards and keeping away from the busy streets, and it appeared to Muggs that the chauffeur was trying to make speed. After a time it turned into the street that led to the river drive, and the speed became higher.

"Drivin' for his health, is he?" Muggs asked himself, and then answered: "Not any, he ain't. That bird's got all the health he needs. It's coin he's after—other folks' coin!"

Mile after mile Muggs followed the car ahead, now creeping up closer when there was traffic, now dropping behind so there would be no suspicion that he was deliberately following. Muggs knew that the roadster he was driving could overhaul the other car at any time. He had made a note of the other car's number, too.

Then they reached the pleasure resort, and the car ahead turned in. Muggs promptly followed.

"Must be out for his health, after all," he mused. "Maybe he's goin' to meet some more of the gang out here. It'd be a good place at that, in all this crowd."

On seeing Landers get out, he parked the roadster and followed his man. Landers walked down to the water front and watched the bathers. Muggs watched him from a corner where he could not be seen. He saw that Landers glanced around now and then, as if to search for some one, or to see whether there was an enemy near.

Then Landers began walking along the shore of the river, and presently turned into a little grove and made his way toward a road that ran through the woods.

"Now we get it!" Muggs said. "Here's where he meets some of the gang. I wish the boss was here!"

Muggs followed him cautiously through the woods, careful not to attract attention. They came to a lane, and Landers turned down it, glanced around, and then began walking faster.

Muggs remained in the woods, but followed as swiftly as he could. He managed to keep Landers in sight. After a time he saw his quarry leave the lane and plunge into the woods again, cut through them, and come out where there was a clearing and an old farmhouse in the midst of a grove of trees.

Crouching behind a clump of brush, Muggs watched Landers stoop and pick up something. The man's back was turned and Muggs could not see what he was doing. Presently he got up, walked to the gate, stood there a moment, and then opened it and passed inside. He took great care, Muggs thought, to see that the gate was closed and latched again.

The valet remained where he was for several minutes, and then crept forward under the brush until he reached the spot where he had seen Landers stoop. He felt around there—and found a telephone.

"Ha!" Muggs said to himself. "This is a funny thing to find around here. He phoned before he opened that gate, too! I've got an idea that fence ain't a pleasant thing to touch, and I ain't goin' to try it until I know. I wish the boss was here!"

He put the telephone back, crept on through the brush, and watched the house. There was nobody in sight.

"I'll bet that's the big crook's headquarters, or one of his branches where he plans things," Muggs told himself. "And I ain't man enough to tackle it alone. The thing for me to do is get back and phone the boss, and get him out here with a gang!"

Muggs started to back through the brush. He heard a step behind him, then whirled and tried to get to his feet. He found himself in the clutches of two men dressed as fishermen.

In his younger days, Muggs had enjoyed a reputation for being an excellent rough-and-tumble fighter. He still retained some of his strength and all his knowledge of how to conduct such a combat. He uttered no word, but went into action.

He kicked, struck, tried to bite and to get his thumbs into the eyes of one of his antagonists, ignoring all rules of fistic combat, striving only to be victor. But he found that he was fighting men who were used to such tactics.

Back and forth across the ground they fought and wrestled, until Muggs' breath was coming in gasps, he was seeing red, and he felt his strength going. Another fisherman crashed through the brush and threw himself into the fray—and Muggs went down from a blow to his chin.

He came back to consciousness to find two of the fishermen bending over him, one of them throwing water in his face. He struggled to get up, but they held him securely. Then he saw that he was not out of doors, but in the house.

"No more fightin' for you just now!" one of the fishermen growled at him.

"Let me up, and I'll show you!" Muggs said. "What you mean jumpin' me like you did?"

"What do you mean by snoopin' around and investigatin' things you ain't got any business investigatin'?"

"I don't remember investigatin' anything. Can't a man bum through the woods any more? Is there a law agin' it?"

"There is in this particular section of the woods," the fisherman replied. "And you needn't try to run any bluff, either. We watched you lookin' at that telephone—and we was watchin' you before that, trailin' a man."

"Yeh?" Muggs asked.

"Yeh! And now you're goin' to do a little explainin'."

"Let's see you make me!" Muggs exclaimed.

"We ain't goin' to try to make yeh. There's another man to do that. You get up and we'll tie your hands behind your back, in case you want to get violent and beat somebody up. And if you start a fight again, we'll just wallop the everlastin' face off you. Get me?"

They lifted Muggs up. He started to struggle, but was no match for them. They held him, and lashed his wrists together behind his back with fish cord. Then they thrust him along a narrow hall and to a door.

One of them pressed a button, and Muggs heard a bell tinkle. Then a buzzer sounded.

"In you go!" one of the fishermen said.

They opened the door and thrust him forward, and he heard the door slammed behind him. Muggs blinked his eyes rapidly, for the hall had been half dark, and the apartment in which he now stood was lighted brilliantly.

He saw a room with expensive furnishings. A long table was in the middle of it, heavy chairs were scattered around, and before him was a man dressed in a black robe, with a black mask on his face, and a flaming star of jet on his hood.

"Greetings, my dear Muggs!" the Black Star said. "I regret it if some of my men handled you roughly, but then you are inclined to violence yourself."

"You—you—" Muggs gasped.

"Be seated, Muggs. You must be fatigued after your recent exertions. I understand that you put up a good fight."

"I'll put up a better one if I ever get a chance at you!" Muggs growled. "I'll show you how to make fun of my boss in the newspapers! You *big* crook!"

"That is not an insult, my dear Muggs, but a compliment. I flatter myself that I am a big crook. Please sit down."

Muggs complied. He was still weak from the fight, and he felt that he wanted to gather what strength he could, for use in case an opportunity presented itself.

"I understand that you followed a certain member of my organization," the Black Star went on. "I have rebuked him for his carelessness. Since you have discovered my location, I cannot allow you your freedom, of course, and have you bring the police down upon me. I make it a point, as perhaps you learned before, to change my headquarters now and then. But I am very comfortable and safe here, and have no intention of moving for some time. So you are to be my guest, Muggs, until I do decide to move."

"That's what *you* say!" Muggs exclaimed.

"I scarcely think you'll escape, Muggs, if that is what is in your mind. And, if you behave yourself, I may show you some very interesting things. I shall feed you well, Muggs, and give you plenty of cigarettes. What more can man desire? I do this because I admire your loyalty to your employer. Perhaps, if I keep you prisoner, and so inform him, he will exert himself and add spice to our little game. Mr. Verbeck hasn't betrayed any great amount of cleverness recently, you know."

"Is that so?" Muggs retorted. "He could, if he wanted to, I guess! It looks as if you don't read the newspapers. My boss ain't in the game any more. He and the chief had a scrap!"

"Oh, my dear Muggs! Give me credit for having some intelligence, and some clever people in my organization. I happen to know that it is all a trick—and not a very clever trick at that. I know the arrangement he made with the chief. Thought I'd take my eyes off him, didn't he? Utter rot!"

"I tell you he had a scrap—"

"If that is so—if Verbeck is no longer trying to capture me—why do you betray so much interest in my affairs?" the Black Star demanded. "Why did you follow my man today? Why did you trail him through the woods? Muggs, your story is weak."

Muggs saw that it was, but he wasn't willing to admit it.

"I didn't say I had quit, did I?" he asked. "Maybe I'm after you on my own hook. There's a fat reward up, ain't there?"

"That's not at all clever, Muggs. But we need talk along this line no more. We understand each other, Muggs. You are my enforced guest for a time, and I trust that you'll appreciate my hospitality. If you start causing trouble, I shall be forced to descend to means I abhor—and use violence!"

"You untie my hands and take off that fool robe, and I'll give you all the violence you want!" Muggs cried. "Maybe I can't fight half a dozen thugs of your gang, but I can handle you, all right, without any help!"

"I fear that I must refuse to accept the challenge, Muggs. I have work to do, and it would be delayed if you happened to lay me up for a few days. Perhaps, some other time—"

"Yellow streak!" Muggs taunted.

"Take care!" the Black Star thundered angrily. "You may go too far, my man!"

"Don't you 'my man' me! Even my boss don't do that, and no

crook's goin' to! Not on your life!"

"Then do not make me lose my temper," the Black Star said. "Go over to that couch and make yourself comfortable, Muggs. You may see and hear some interesting things. Since you are to be my guest for some time, until a certain thing is accomplished, I do not care how much you learn. I have an idea that some of my people are about to report."

Muggs, a sudden gleam in his eye, got up and went over to the couch. It was like the Black Star to let him overhear orders and commands; and there always was a chance that he could escape and give the alarm. He needed rest now to gather his strength. He would wait, learn all that he could, catch the Black Star off guard as soon as possible, and effect an escape.

CHAPTER XIX

IMPORTANT INFORMATION

The Black Star watched him closely as he sat down on the couch and tried to make himself comfortable, which was a difficult thing for him to do with his wrists lashed behind his back.

"Muggs," he said, "where did you pick up Landers?"

"What you talkin' about?"

"You know very well. You followed Landers out here, and some of my men saw you trailing him, saw you find the telephone. You know Landers well, for he was one of my old organization and escaped when Verbeck caught me and scattered my men."

"What difference does it make?" Muggs asked. "I picked him up, didn't I?"

"I give you credit for it, Muggs. But just where did you pick him up? If any of my men are careless, I want to know it. Was it Landers' carelessness or your cleverness?"

"I saw the big stiff walkin' along the street and gettin' into an auto, and trailed him," Muggs said.

"Very good!" replied the Black Star.

Muggs felt sure that there was a note of keen satisfaction in the Black Star's speech, and he guessed the reason for it. The master crook thought Muggs meant that he had seen Landers getting into the touring car. He was worrying for fear Muggs knew of his visit to the hotel.

"Some more of the gang there—them Whaley women!" Muggs told himself.

A bell on the wall tinkled, and the Black Star hurried to one end of the room and pressed a button.

"I must ask you to remain perfectly quiet, Muggs," he warned.

"You may see all you like, since you'll never be able to give out the information soon enough to hurt my plans, but you must not speak when any of my people are in the room. Be good, Muggs, and I'll have your hands untied after a while."

The door at the other end of the room was opened, and a robed and masked man came in and went to the blackboard. He regarded Muggs carefully, but the Black Star motioned for him to proceed.

"Number Two," he wrote.

"Countersign?"

"Bennington."

"Report," wrote the Black Star, and as Muggs watched they held their conversation on the blackboards, writing and erasing, neither speaking a word.

"Invitation list includes all prominent and wealthy persons in the city and some from out of town," wrote Number Two.

"Date remains the same?"

"Yes; tomorrow night."

"How about detectives?"

"Four—two men and two women—from the usual agency. We cannot handle any of them by the customary means, but they will not be hard to get out of the way."

"Make arrangements for doing so," wrote the Black Star. "If you need help, ask for it tomorrow morning. What arrangements have been made about refreshments?"

"A caterer is to serve them. Two of the waiters are our men."

"Good! Anything special regarding possible loot?"

"Since it is such an affair, all the women are likely to wear their most expensive jewels," wrote Number Two. "Social rivalry that exists at present will tend toward this."

"That is all for the present. Retire!"

Number Two erased what was written, bowed, and backed through the door. The Black Star glanced at a little clock that stood on the table before him.

"I have a few minutes before the next man reports, Muggs," he said, "and so I'll be glad to explain in part. I presume you have heard of our fair city's society leader, Mrs. Richard Branniton?"

"Sure!" said Muggs.

"She is giving quite an affair tomorrow evening at her palatial residence, Muggs. Her husband, if you happen to remember, was the district attorney who prosecuted me when I was on trial recently. At this reception and ball, she is to entertain two prominent diplomats who are visiting in the city. The cream of the city's wealth and society will be present, Muggs. It will be some party!"

"Well, what about it? I ain't invited," Muggs growled.

"You may be a guest at that, Muggs; I may take you with me."

"Oh! You're invited, are you?" Muggs asked sarcastically.

"No; but I am going. It isn't quite the thing to go to an affair to which you have received no invitation, yet I intend doing it, Muggs. There are times when I am not strictly conventional, as you may have guessed. I am going, Muggs—and I am going to take about twenty or thirty of my best men with me."

"It'll sure be some party, then!"

"There will be a few exciting moments, I doubt not. You see, Muggs, the ladies will wear fortunes in jewels—and I love jewels. Besides, they are worth money when properly marketed. I shall strip Mrs. Richard Branniton's guests of their precious jewels. This will injure that lady socially to a certain extent, and thereby hurt Mr. Branniton, who was quite nasty at the time of my trial."

"He wasn't nasty enough!"

"Oh, well, you are prejudiced, Muggs. And the jewels are not all, Muggs. We are going to abduct those two famous diplomats and hold them for ransom. Is not that a master stroke? I certainly am a big crook, am I not?"

"You can't get away with it!" Muggs said.

"Nonsense! We have a place prepared to which we shall take them. We have a method of collecting the ransom when it is paid—a safe method. And it will be paid, Muggs—two hundred thousand dollars for each man. You see, they are here on international business, and very important business at that. It will be necessary to secure their release at once. If it is not accomplished, there might be trouble with a certain other country. Oh, we have it all planned, Muggs, and the job will not be so difficult as others I have handled."

"You go to monkeyin' with the government, and you'll get yours good and plenty!" Muggs warned him.

"I fear no government, Muggs! I tell you, our plans are perfect. The ransom will be paid within three days."

The Black Star went to the table, opened a drawer, and consulted a memorandum book. Again the little bell on the wall tinkled. Once more the Black Star pressed a button and a robed and masked man entered and stepped up to the blackboard.

"Number Four," he wrote.

"Countersign?"

"Delaware."

"Report," wrote the Black Star.

"Lord Sambery and Sir Burton Banks will arrive tomorrow morning at ten o'clock and be taken at once to the Branniton residence. They will have luncheon there, and then be taken for a drive through the city."

"How many will be in the party?"

"Just the luncheon party—perhaps fifteen."

"What else?" the Black Star wrote.

"Diplomats will return to the Branniton residence and remain for the reception. Arrangements you ordered have been made."

"Good!" the Black Star wrote. "Report at usual time

tomorrow for additional orders. Retire!"

The man bowed and backed through the door. The Black Star turned toward Muggs again.

"Oh, it is a wonderful organization, my dear Muggs!" he said. "It is far more wonderful than the one I had before."

"I ain't carin' much about it!" Muggs said. "These blamed cords are cuttin' my wrists, and my nose itches and I can't scratch it!"

"Suppose I untie you?"

"You'd better watch me, if you do."

"Ah! That is what I thought," the master crook said. "You retain your violent nature, I see. One of these days you will realize the futility of it, Muggs."

"I'll realize my life ambition by beatin' you up!" Muggs replied. "You goin' to take off these cords?"

"Not that. But I'll have your wrists tied in front, so you will be able to scratch your nose," said the Black Star, chuckling.

He opened the hall door and called two of the fishermen into the room. For some reason, it appeared, the fishermen did not wear robes and masks before the Black Star, and evidently did not care that Muggs saw their faces.

The master rogue issued his orders, and the two men untied Muggs' wrists, lashed them again in front of him, and then hurried away.

"Now you may scratch your nose," the Black Star said. "I suppose you'll be trying to free yourself, too. Allow me to tell you, Muggs, that you'd not get very far if you did."

"I noticed Landers wait until the current was turned off that fence," Muggs said.

"Ah! You know about that, do you? But that is only one thing among many, my dear Muggs. I'd advise you to be a contented prisoner for the time being. You'll gain nothing by trying to escape."

"Well, how long are you goin' to keep me here?"

"Until I move to my next headquarters, I said."

"And when'll that be?"

"In two weeks possibly. Until then, Muggs, you must be one of us. When I move, I'll have you dropped somewhere in town, and you can tell Verbeck and the newspapers all you saw and heard. You'll be getting your picture on the front page, Muggs."

Again the bell tinkled, and once more a robed and masked man entered and stepped to the blackboard. He gave his number and countersign.

"Report," wrote the Black Star.

"It is as you thought—Verbeck is still after us."

"Anything more about Verbeck?"

"He visited his fiancée this afternoon, and afterward took a taxi and got out at a busy corner. He remained there for some time, and then went home. He acted as if he was waiting for somebody."

"Anything else?"

"Verbeck's roadster is at the resort down the river, and has been there for several hours. We didn't see Verbeck."

"His chauffeur left it there; that is his chauffeur on the couch," the Black Star wrote.

The man at the other blackboard turned and regarded Muggs through the slits in his mask. Muggs knew what that meant. Here was a man who was not acquainted with him, but hereafter he would know Roger Verbeck's chauffeur when he saw him.

"Anything else?" the Black Star wrote again.

"Sheriff Kowen is swearing in more deputies, and some of them are experienced officers who have retired."

"Anything from police headquarters?"

"Nothing, sir, except that the chief is keeping in communication with Verbeck through some third person. We have not located this person yet."

"Do so as soon as possible, and let me know the result over the telephone," the Black Star wrote. "That is all!"

The masked man bowed and backed through the door. Once more the master crook faced Muggs.

"You see, my dear Muggs, I find out everything," he said. "I could tell you what Roger Verbeck had to eat at breakfast this morning. How can a man like Verbeck expect to win against an organization such as mine?"

"He'll win, all right!" Muggs growled. "He'll get you before he quits!"

CHAPTER XX

ON THE TRAIL

Having received Muggs' startling telephone message that he was trailing Landers, the master crook's trusted lieutenant, Roger Verbeck left his fiancée, hurried from the apartment house, engaged a taxicab, and had the chauffeur drive him to the New Nortonia Hotel as quickly as possible.

He got out of the cab half a block away from the hotel entrance, and looked around for the roadster and Muggs, but failed to find them. Verbeck's enthusiasm began to die instantly. He had hoped to find Muggs still there, to join him, possibly to follow Landers until he met more of the gang.

For half an hour Verbeck loitered around the corner, and then he decided that Muggs had been forced to go on alone, that Landers had left the hotel and Muggs had been afraid to remain behind, lest he lose his man. So Verbeck went home to await another telephone message, as he had told Muggs he would do.

At the end of an hour, he had received no message. He paced the floor, consumed several cigarettes, and began worrying a bit about it. That Muggs was the sort of man to rush into trouble, Verbeck knew well. Muggs was inclined to fight first and think about things afterward. If Muggs had located Landers, and Landers did not know it, there were several possibilities.

Muggs might have followed the Black Star's lieutenant to the master crook's headquarters, or been decoyed to some other place and made prisoner. It was the silence of Muggs that bothered Roger Verbeck. Surely he could have managed to get to a telephone within an hour, Verbeck thought.

Verbeck waited for another hour, and still had received no message from Muggs. He called a certain number himself, and spoke at length to the man who answered him, and who would relay the message to the chief of police by word of mouth.

"Muggs spotted one of the Black Star's men and started to follow him," Verbeck said. "He hasn't reported to me since. Tell the chief to have all the men on the force look for my roadster, as Muggs was driving it. Muggs may need help. And wherever that roadster is found, some of the Black Star's men may be in the neighborhood. Understand? Possibly Muggs has not had a chance to communicate with me. He may be a prisoner."

Roger Verbeck continued to pace the floor of his living room and wait. Half an hour afterward his telephone bell rang, and he hastened to answer, hoping that the call was from Muggs, and that it would lead to the apprehension of the Black Star or some of his people.

"Mr. Verbeck?" asked a voice.

"Yes."

"Good afternoon. I trust that you are in excellent health. This is the Black Star speaking!"

"Well, what do you want?" Verbeck growled.

"Aren't you rather discourteous this afternoon? I have important news for you, too. Your man, Muggs is making me an extended visit at my headquarters. That is what I wished to let you know. He followed a member of my band, and stumbled upon the place. Some more of my men subdued him. I must keep him here now, of course, but I shall take good care of him, I assure you."

"You'd better!" Verbeck said.

"And your splendid roadster, Mr. Verbeck—Muggs was driving it, as you know. I have had one of my men take it downtown and leave it in front of the public library. You'd better hurry there and get it, or you'll be fined for leaving it standing in the street so long. I couldn't leave it where Muggs deserted it, you know; that might have given a clew to my whereabouts."

Then the Black Star terminated the conversation abruptly,

and Roger Verbeck slammed the receiver into its hook. Verbeck had hoped that the discovery of his roadster would put the police and himself on the right trail.

Once more Verbeck called the go-between, and had the chief of police informed of his conversation with the Black Star. Then he called the office of the sheriff.

"That you, Kowen?" he asked. "This is Roger Verbeck. It has been given out, as you know, that I am no longer working with the police, and I am not certain whether the Black Star believes it, or not, though I scarcely think that he does. So I don't want to call on the police for help just now. I wish you'd hurry right up here to my place, Kowen. I've got an important clew. And have one of your men go to the corner by the New Nortonia Hotel and wait there for us, will you? We may need him."

"I'll send a good man there, and I'll be with you in fifteen minutes!" Kowen declared.

The sheriff was as good as his word. A quarter of an hour later he was sitting before the table in Verbeck's living room, puffing at a cigar Verbeck had given him.

"Well, Verbeck, what's the idea?" he wanted to know. "If you've got a clew to that crook's whereabouts, for Heaven's sake let's get busy on it. If we don't land him pretty quick, the dear public will be running us out of town."

"I visited my fiancée this afternoon," Verbeck said, "and left Muggs sitting in the roadster. A few minutes later, the clerk in the apartment house telephoned up to me that Muggs had said to tell me he had seen a man, and would call me later.

"I knew what that meant, of course. We had been watching continually for some of the Black Star's old people. So I waited eagerly for his message, and finally it came. The man he had been trailing was Landers, one of the Black Star's trusted lieutenants. Muggs said he had gone to the New Nortonia Hotel, and was visiting a couple of women named Whaley, who had room 256 there."

"Some clew!" said the sheriff.

"Wait! I told Muggs I'd be right over, but that if Landers left the hotel to follow him and call me at home later. When I got over there, Muggs was gone. I came home, and waited a couple of hours, but got no message from him. Finally the Black Star called me up. He said he had Muggs at his headquarters and would keep him a prisoner for a time. Muggs stumbled into some sort of a trap, it seems. We don't know where the crook's headquarters are, of course. But I'm inclined to investigate room 256, at the New Nortonia Hotel, sheriff. What do you think about it?"

"I should say we will investigate it!" Kowen declared. "If the Black Star's lieutenant visits the people in that room, I want to know who those people are."

"Muggs said they were two sisters named Whaley. That means nothing, of course. They probably belong to the Black Star's gang. They may be important, or they may be merely mediums through whom members of the band receive messages and orders from one another. Now, we want to go about this thing carefully, sheriff. We ought to investigate, but we don't care to have them know of it until we learn all there is to be learned."

"I get the idea," the sheriff agreed. "Let's go!"

"We'll wait until after dark—which will not be more than a couple of hours," Verbeck said. "I'll have some dinner sent up here, and that will help kill the time. I visit that hotel now and then myself—have a bachelor friend who lives there. So the clerk and elevator boy will think nothing of it if we go right up without being announced. You leave the little details for me, Kowen. All I want is your official support—and your good right arm, of course, in case we get into a bit of trouble."

"You can have 'em both!" the sheriff said.

Verbeck ordered the dinner, and the sheriff indulged in a

moment of luxury. Never before had he smoked such cigars or eaten such food. Being a young man of fortune was a good thing, Kowen decided. He didn't see why Roger Verbeck should go around trying to round up a master crook when he was so comfortable at home.

Night descended, and they left the apartment and the building by means of a rear stairs. Verbeck explained that it was probable that the Black Star had somebody watching the place.

"We don't want them to think we know anything about that hotel," he said. "We may lose our chance to nab some of them if they get an idea we are on the right trail."

They walked through back streets, keeping in the shadows as much as possible, and finally reached the hostelry. There, of course, they had to enter boldly. Verbeck nodded to the clerk and hurried to the elevator with the sheriff at his heels. They ascended to the fourth floor, where Verbeck's friend, Lawrence, lived.

"We're here on business connected with a gentleman known to fame as the Black Star, Lawrence," Verbeck said, finding his friend in his suite.

"Good Lord! Think I'm a member of his gang?" Lawrence asked.

"Scarcely, or we'd not be taking you into our confidence," Verbeck replied. "Be a good boy, now, and help us, will you?"

"Surely! That big crook nipped my aunt's diamonds the last time he was on a rampage, and she never got them back. Just give me a chance at him. Those stones were to have been mine some day."

"In that case, you probably want revenge," said Verbeck, laughing. "Now, answer a few questions. You've lived here for three or four years and should know something about the place."

"I know all about it," Lawrence said.

"Where is room 256?"

"Ah! I had that room when I first came here, before I could

get a suite. It's on the second floor, directly beneath us a couple of stories, with a fire escape running past its principal window."

"Of course there would be a fire escape," said Verbeck. "There are times when fire escapes are handy things. Lawrence, do you know the people who have that room now? I understand a couple of sisters live there—Whaley by name."

"I've seen one of them many times—sour-looking old girl about forty. Freeze you with a glance, and all that sort of thing— one of those women a man always dodges."

"Sure she is about forty?"

"Great Scott, don't I know the sex? Can't I guess a woman's age nine times out of ten? Aren't half the girls in town mad at me now because I always insist on doing it, and telling the truth about my guesses? She's forty, and she's fat—not plump, but fat—and she always looks as if she was ready to bite."

"Well, that description doesn't mean anything in my young life," Verbeck said. "I had hoped for something different. How about the other sister?"

"I've glanced at her a couple of times, but I haven't seen her at all recently. Maybe she's ill."

"What does she look like—that's what I want to know."

"Um!" said Lawrence. "Grace of a gazelle, my boy. Would have made advances, my boy, if the other hadn't frozen me with a glance."

"Hair?"

"Auburn—distinct auburn, the shade I most prefer—and plenty of it. Eyes, a sort of gray—don't know exactly what you'd call 'em. And the girl can wear clothes. There's a subtle perfume about her, my boy—"

"And you only glanced at her a couple of times, eh? How old do you say she is?" Verbeck asked.

"Thirty," Lawrence replied. "Five feet six; weighs about a

hundred and twenty-five, has magnificent shoulders—"

"I knew it!" Verbeck cried.

"Can you place her?" Kowen asked.

"It is only a guess, of course," said Verbeck. "But I think I know who she is. And I'm sure you'd be interested in meeting her, Kowen. You'll take such a fancy to her that you'll probably want to take her to jail and put her into a cage. Kowen, is that man of yours at the corner, do you suppose?"

"If he isn't, he'll be fired pretty quick!"

"Go out and find him, and plant him beneath that fire escape. Tell him to nab anybody, man or woman, who tries to go down it. A person can go down that escape to the parlor on the first floor, you know, step through a window there, and walk out the front door of the hotel. Then you hurry right back here, Kowen."

The sheriff grasped his hat and hurried from the suite. Verbeck lighted a cigarette, looking toward the ceiling and smiled.

"I say, what is this all about?" Lawrence demanded. "Let me in on it, will you? I haven't had a bit of excitement for ages. I'm getting stale, man."

"Callow youths such as yourself should not run into danger," Verbeck explained.

"Confound it, I'm no callow youth. I'm only three years younger than you."

"But I have had experience, Lawrence. Restrain yourself for a few minutes, and you may see some excitement. But don't ask questions at the present time. I hate answering questions. We must wait until the sheriff comes back."

CHAPTER XXI

A TENSE MOMENT

Sheriff Kowen located his deputy instantly, and gave the man his orders. Then the sheriff showed that there was real stuff in him. He did not turn around and reënter the hotel by the main door. It had occurred to him that, if any of the Black Star's men were on watch, they might get suspicious if they saw him around the place too much.

Kowen walked down the street, entered a cigar store, made a purchase, and sauntered on around the block. He darted into the alley and reached the rear of the hotel building, and went in at the servants' entrance when he was sure that he was not being observed.

He exhibited his badge to the first man he met, and was shown how to reach the rear stairs. By this means he mounted to the fourth floor and so reached Lawrence's suite again.

"My man's ready," he reported to Verbeck. "If anybody gets down that fire escape and away, it'll be peculiar. That man can handle bad ones as easily as others handle infants."

"What are you going to do?" Lawrence inquired.

"The sheriff and I are going to investigate room 256 and the inhabitants thereof," Verbeck replied. "We are going to walk up to the door and knock. If we find, when the door is opened, that we have made a mistake, we shall apologize and say something about knocking at the wrong door. If we find that we have not made a mistake, there probably will be fireworks."

"I always did like fireworks," Lawrence said. "Do I get to see these?"

"You may look from your window all you please," Verbeck said. "But we can't have you with us just now. There may be nothing in this, and there may be a lot. Ready, sheriff?"

"You know it!" the sheriff answered.

"Allow me to suggest that you put your revolver in your coat pocket, and put your hand in the same pocket and grasp the revolver. Don't show the weapon, of course, until we are sure that we are right. We don't want to frighten innocent persons, if it can be avoided."

"Who do you think is in that room, Verbeck?" Kowen asked.

"Let us see!" Verbeck replied.

Ignoring Lawrence's demand that he be allowed to accompany them, they left the suite and walked slowly down the stairs. They reached the second floor, and went along the hall until they reached No. 256. There they stopped, listened. They could hear somebody talking inside.

Verbeck knocked smartly and then stepped close to the door, the sheriff at his side. The voices within were stilled, but nobody answered. Verbeck knocked again, and suddenly the door was thrown open.

Sheriff Kowen gasped, and his revolver was whipped from his pocket. Roger Verbeck merely chuckled. The woman who had opened the door gave a little screech and tried to close it again, but Verbeck's foot prevented. They thrust her back, stepped inside, and closed the door behind them.

"Good evening, Miss Blanchard!" said Sheriff Kowen. "I tell the truth when I say that I am delighted to see you!"

"And it is some time since I have had the pleasure of greeting The Princess," Verbeck added. "Pardon the peculiar manner of this call, but we felt that it was necessary."

The face of the woman before them had gone white, and now it flushed. She stepped backward into the room as they advanced. Sitting near the window was another woman—fat and forty—and she sprang to her feet.

"What is the meaning of this intrusion?" she cried. "I shall call the office—"

"Calm yourself, madam!" Verbeck told her. "I have not the pleasure of your acquaintance, but I find you in bad company, and that is sufficient."

"Yes, and I've got a couple of dandy cells down at the county jail!" the sheriff said. "They're all cleaned and waiting for you. Hot and cold water, and eats three times a day. I've stopped raiding gambling dens for the moment and am taking up another line of work."

He glared at Mamie Blanchard, who was standing close to the table and glaring back at him.

"Sit down, Miss Blanchard!" Verbeck said. "We are going to have a short conversation. And kindly do not attempt any foolish move. I dislike to fight a woman, but at times it seems to be necessary."

Mamie Blanchard sat down. Verbeck could tell, by glancing at her face, that she had regained her composure—that she was clever, dangerous, a woman to be watched closely.

"Well, what is it?" she demanded.

"I don't suppose you'll do as I ask, but I am going to give you a chance," Verbeck said. "I want some information about the Black Star."

"I don't know anything about him. I was in his old gang, as you are aware. I supposed you had come to arrest me for that. He didn't see fit to include me in his new organization, because you knew me, I suppose."

"That statement is not at all clever of you," said Verbeck. "You are talking to men who know better. You helped engineer his escape, didn't you?"

"Since you know, I did. That is, I got the sheriff to raid the gambling house, and decoyed him to the little cottage. The Black Star gave me that much to do because I needed money.

But that is all."

"You mean your work for him is done?" Verbeck asked.

"Yes."

"You're not in touch with him any more?"

"No."

"Um! And yet Landers, his trusted lieutenant, is a frequent visitor here."

"Perhaps that is for personal reasons," said Mamie Blanchard. "We saw each other a great deal when we were in the old gang, and we are—well, interested in each other to a certain extent."

"I wish that I could believe your story of a fond romance, but I am afraid that I cannot," Verbeck said. "Let us put the cards on the table. You know, Miss Blanchard, that it is only a question of time when the Black Star will be recaptured and his band scattered or sent to jail. It will go easier with you personally if you give me the information I desire; and please do not waste time and breath by saying that you do not know. Where is the Black Star's headquarters?"

"I don't know—and that is the truth."

"Possibly it is the truth, but you report to him through somebody. I suppose it is Landers, since he calls here so much. When will Landers be here again?"

"I don't know."

"What do you know about the Black Star's plans for the future?"

"I don't know anything about them," said Mamie Blanchard.

"She knows, all right, but she'll not talk," the sheriff declared. "Might as well haul them both to jail, I guess. There's an old charge against this Blanchard woman, and we can hold the other on suspicion while we make an investigation."

"You dare take me to jail!" shouted the fat-and-forty lady.

"Tut, tut!" said Sheriff Kowen.

The sheriff did not take his eyes off Mamie Blanchard. He was aware that she was clever, and he was watching for her to make some move. He watched her hands particularly.

Verbeck bent forward in his chair again. "It will be a great deal better for you to talk," he cautioned.

"I've said all that I am going to say!" Mamie Blanchard declared. "If you want to take me to jail, take me! The Black Star will get me out, and he'll take pay from the city because I was arrested!"

"You think you can bluff me with a speech like that?" Kowen demanded. "Not in the least, young woman! You do not seem to appreciate what you are facing."

"And you," she said, "do not seem to appreciate what is behind you at this moment!"

"Trying to get me to turn around, so you can make some sort of a move, are you?" the sheriff asked. "That's old stuff—telling a man to look behind him."

"There is something behind you, all right," she said.

A man's voice greeted them from the rear.

"I've got both of you covered! Drop that gun, sheriff!"

Both the sheriff and Verbeck suddenly felt something pressing against the backs of their necks. Each knew what it was—the muzzle of a weapon.

"Drop it!" said the voice again.

The sheriff dropped his gun. He knew it was the only thing to do when another man had the drop on him.

"Sit still! Don't turn around!" said the voice again.

Suddenly the air about the two men was filled with pungent fumes. Their heads dropped forward. Once more a vapor gun had done its work, and done it instantly and well.

* * * *

Roger Verbeck and Sheriff Kowen returned to consciousness to find that they were bound and gagged and lashed to chairs placed against the wall. The two women were still in the room.

Landers was there, too.

"You fail again, Verbeck," he said. "You must be losing your cleverness, as the Black Star says. You enter a room as you entered this, and sit down and turn your back upon a closet without examining it first. It was very easy to overcome you after that. I didn't look for any brains in the sheriff, of course, but I did in you.

"The question now is what to do with you. We have been discussing it while you were unconscious. Had I my way, you'd be put where you'd bother us no longer, but the Black Star will not countenance that sort of violence. He is tender-hearted in some things, as you know.

"It appears that you have discovered our little retreat here, and so we cannot remain. These ladies will have to go out with me, without even taking their clothes and toilet articles, and not return. It is a nuisance to find another hiding place, but there are plenty of them in the city. We shall have to leave you here, of course. I promise to telephone the hotel later, and have you released.

"Thought you'd get some information, did you? Let me tell you, Roger Verbeck, that you'll never catch the Black Star this time. And he'll strip the city before he is through. He has planned something for tomorrow night that will not only startle the city, but the entire country as well. There is not a chance in the world of you or the police or the sheriff's force preventing it—or doing anything after it has been accomplished."

Landers motioned to the women, and they went to the closet for hats and cloaks.

"I don't see the sense of leaving everything," Mamie Blanchard said. "We can say at the office that I am going away for a few days, but that my sister will remain. They'll think that you are merely taking me to the train. At least, I can take a bag. I can put a lot of things in that."

"Very well; perhaps that would be best," Landers agreed.

"Take your time, my dear. There is no need to rush things. We are not likely to be disturbed here. You'd better put on a heavy veil, too. There may be a deputy or two around the hotel, and some of them might recognize you. I'll telephone for a taxi just before we go down."

The two women began packing the bag, while Landers turned his back on his prisoners, went to the window and looked down at the street.

Verbeck and the sheriff glanced at each other helplessly. There was small chance that they would be able to trail Landers and the women if they got away now; and after this they would keep in hiding better. It appeared that the Black Star's good luck was with him yet.

Verbeck tugged at his bonds, but knew instantly that there was small hope of freeing himself. If he did, Landers held the advantage. But it was Verbeck's idea that he could get free at least soon after the others left the room, and make an effort to trace them.

Landers turned away from the window.

"Verbeck, your man trailed me this afternoon," he said. "He saw me come into this hotel, I suppose, and found out what room I visited. He's out at the Black Star's headquarters now, a pampered guest; but when I get a chance, I'm going to give him what's coming to him. He was the cause of my getting a rebuke from the Black Star."

"I wish you'd rap that sheriff on the head," Mamie Blanchard remarked. "He's a nuisance!"

"The Black Star will not stand for work like that, and you know it," Landers replied. "Besides, the sheriff is harmless; we have little to fear from him."

Sheriff Kowen's face grew purple with wrath, and he gurgled behind his gag.

Mamie Blanchard was packing the bag, and her stout companion was gathering the things to put into it. Verbeck continued working at the bonds about his wrists. The cords were cutting through the flesh, but he did not desist. He knew that every second would be precious as soon as Landers and the two women left the room.

He stopped for an instant, because the exertion was tiring him, and his wrists pained so much. He saw that Kowen was trying to get free, too, and knew that he was making a failure of it. Landers had done his work well; it was evident that the man was an expert at binding and gagging.

Presently Landers came over, inspected their bonds, and laughed.

"You are only mutilating your wrists, Mr. Verbeck," he said. "I assure you that you will be unable to get free. I promise to call up the hotel within an hour or so, and tell them to come up and release you. It will get into the newspapers, of course—and the public will have another laugh at your expense—but you should be used to that by this time, you and the sheriff both. The town should give us credit for handing them a laugh now and then, as well as thrills."

The sheriff gurgled behind his gag again.

Verbeck looked past him to the window at which was the landing of the fire escape. He saw a shadow there, and looked away. Then he glanced back again, a new hope born in his breast. Once more he observed a shadow, and then a man's face showed for an instant as he peered inside. The man was his friend, Lawrence.

Lawrence had fussed and fumed for ten minutes after Verbeck and the sheriff had left. He had opened the window by the fire escape, and had looked down. The shade at the window in the room on the second floor was only partially drawn, and Lawrence could see the light streaming out.

"Wonder what those chaps are up to?" he asked himself. "Mean of Verbeck not to let me in on it. Ought to hear some sort of an explosion soon, I fancy. Maybe there'll be a row—give the hotel a bad name—beastly mess!"

He waited for half an hour longer, hanging out of the window and watching below. He saw nothing, heard nothing. At the foot of the fire escape a man was standing—the sheriff's deputy.

Then the lust for adventure was born in Lawrence's bosom. He chuckled at the very idea. He opened the window wider, and got out on the landing of the fire escape.

He began slowly descending the ladder, round by round, passed the landing on the third floor, and continued to the second. He went close to the window, and looked in.

He saw the sheriff and Roger Verbeck bound and gagged and lashed in their chairs. He saw Landers walking around the room, a revolver in his hand, and the two women packing the bag.

"Great Scott!" he breathed. "Verbeck and Kowen seem to have come a cropper! Prisoners, eh? Ought to give them a bit of help, I suppose. Can't let that other chap get away with this, of course."

Landers walked toward the window, and Lawrence drew back from it. He waited a moment, then glanced in again—and met Verbeck's eyes. Lawrence nodded his head. He went to the end of the fire-escape landing and looked down at the deputy, who had been watching him carefully, remembering his orders. He took a notebook from his pocket, and a pencil from another, and scribbled a message:

> Come up quick! Man and two women in room have Verbeck and sheriff bound and gagged. They are packing bag and preparing to leave. I can't tackle this alone. I'm Verbeck's friend, Lawrence. Either come up the fire escape or go inside and to room 256 and nab them at the door, and I'll watch here.

He tossed the note down, and the deputy picked it up and read it. The deputy was not certain just what to do. If he went inside the hotel he would disregard the sheriff's orders, which had been to watch the fire escape. So the deputy decided to climb.

He sprang up and caught the bottom of the iron ladder, reached the first landing, and worked his way up, watching Lawrence closely, a weapon held ready if Lawrence proved to be foe instead of friend. Lawrence glanced inside the room again, and gestured to Verbeck that he had reason to hope.

CHAPTER XXII

ON THE ROOF

Lawrence peered through the window again, as the deputy made his way up the fire escape. The two women were putting on their hats and veils. Landers had stepped before Verbeck and Sheriff Kowen again, and was speaking to them.

"I shall report all this to the Black Star," he was saying, "and he will take great pleasure in relating it to the newspapers. We must give the dear public another chance to laugh, as I said before. I regret that the chief of police is not with you."

Just then the deputy reached the landing of the fire escape, and looked at Lawrence closely.

"We haven't any time to lose," Lawrence whispered. "Look inside the room."

Lawrence, realizing that the deputy was suspicious of him, stepped back, and the other man took a step forward and glanced through the window.

"I want to get in on this; Roger Verbeck is a friend of mine!" Lawrence declared. "What are we going to do?"

He looked through the window again as he spoke. Mamie Blanchard had picked up the bag and stepped to the door. The older woman was following her. Landers was preparing to leave.

"Don't worry, gentlemen," he was saying. "I'll notify the hotel to release you within an hour or so, I'll turn out the lights, of course."

The deputy waited no longer. He appeared to be convinced now that Lawrence was acting in good faith. He sprang forward, thrust his foot through the window, kicked at the glass repeatedly, rolled up the shade and sprang into the room. Lawrence was only a pace behind him, and eager for the fray.

Landers and his companions had whirled around at the first crash of the glass. One of the women screamed. Landers cursed, sprang to the light switch, and snapped off the lights. The door was hurled open, and the two women fled into the hall. Landers fired one shot from the vapor gun, sprang after them, stopped long enough to turn the key in the lock on the outside, and hurried after his female confederates to the elevator.

Lawrence and the deputy charged across the room, trying to keep from breathing, from inhaling those poisonous fumes. The deputy hurled himself at the door in an effort to break it down. But it was well braced against the woodwork outside, and resisted his efforts.

Lawrence staggered back to the window and took great gulps of the fresh air. Then he whirled around again, turned on the lights and began fumbling at Verbeck's bonds. Verbeck and the sheriff were weak, but the fumes of the vapor gun had not rendered them unconscious. The draft from the broken window had prevented that.

Lawrence tore the gags from the mouths of the bound men, and worked at the fastenings again.

"Down the fire escape!" Kowen shrieked to his deputy. "They called for a taxi. If you see a cop, get him to help. We'll be after you in a minute!"

The deputy darted to the window, and went down the fire escape with the agility of a monkey. Verbeck and Kowen, freed of their bonds at last, got upon their feet. Since it seemed impossible to break down the door leading to the corridor, Verbeck hurled himself against the one opening into an adjoining room. It crashed in, and they staggered into the apartment, startling a man who was dressing there.

"Officers—after crooks!" Kowen gasped.

They flung the hall door open, and rushed out. Lawrence was not far behind them. Verbeck ran at once to the elevators and glanced at the indicators above the doors.

"All at the bottom except one—and that is almost at the top," he gasped. "They surely haven't had time to get to the ground floor, unless they just happened to catch an elevator on the fly, or else went down the stairs."

The sheriff made no reply; already he was dashing down the wide, marble stairs. He reached the floor below, gave the lobby a single glance, and then hurried to the elevators.

"Two women and a man just come down?" he asked.

"Nobody's come down for the last ten minutes or so," the starter replied. "What's the row?"

The deputy had charged in from the street.

"They haven't come this way!" he said. "The taxicab is still waiting for them in front."

"Around to the alley!" the sheriff commanded. "Watch every exit there!"

The hotel manager was on the scene by this time.

"What is the disturbance about?" he demanded.

"We're after some of the Black Star's gang," the sheriff replied.

"In my house?"

"Yes; and they've been living here for some time, if you want to know. I thought this was an exclusive place, where a tenant had to have all sorts of references. Those two women who call themselves Whaley—"

"Why, they are all right!"

"Are they?" asked the sheriff. "One side!"

He took up a position whence he could watch both the stairs and the elevators. The deputy had hurried to the alley. Two policemen came in from the street, and the hotel detective put in an appearance. Kowen took instant command of the situation.

"Let nobody leave the building for the present—nobody!" he commanded. "Let nobody pass out unless either Verbeck or I give them permission!"

Kowen sprang up the wide stairs again. He reached the second floor, and stopped to listen. He heard no sound of pursuit or combat. The elevator came down from above, and the sheriff stopped it.

"Take two women and a man up?" he asked.

"Yes, sir," said the operator.

"Know them?"

"Miss Whaley and—"

"That's enough! Where did they go?"

"To the roof. They said they wanted to take a look at the city, as one of the ladies was going away."

"I'll go up and take a look myself!" the sheriff said. "And give us a little speed!"

The boy whizzed the elevator to the top floor; he didn't know what it was all about, but he sensed excitement.

"You take that flight of stairs to the roof," he explained. "There is a door at the top."

Kowen did not wait to thank him. He rushed for the stairs— and ran into Verbeck and Lawrence.

"They're on the roof!" Verbeck said. "And the door is locked, of course!"

"Then we've got them!" Kowen declared. "It's a cinch they can't get down!"

"Don't forget that we had the Black Star on a roof once, and he got down," Verbeck reminded him. "I just examined that door; it's a strong one."

"Why use the door?" Lawrence asked quietly. "I know this building pretty well, and I can get to the roof without going through the door at all."

"How?" Verbeck asked.

"I can get through that window, hang to the cornice, and

draw myself up."

"You'd fall, man!" Kowen declared. "You'd kill yourself!"

"I can do it!" Verbeck exclaimed. "It isn't a bit harder than things I'm doing in the gymnasium all the time."

He hurried to the window, opened it, and looked at the cornice above.

"Don't try it!" Kowen said. "It's twelve stories to the pavement below, Mr. Verbeck."

"But I'm not going to fall!"

"They're not worth it—"

"What? The Black Star's first lieutenant, and the cleverest woman in his band? I'm going up! You go to the door at the head of the stairs and pound against it—make them think you are trying to break through—attract their attention! Do it now!"

He removed his shoes as he spoke. Kowen made a last protest, which drew no reply from Verbeck except a grin. Then the sheriff and Lawrence went back up the steps, and began pounding against the door.

Verbeck was cool and collected now. He realized the task that was before him, and he knew the danger he would be running. A fall would mean death on the pavement twelve floors below. Verbeck was thankful that it was dark.

Once more he looked up at the cornice. Then he got through the window, balanced himself on the sill, and reached up and grasped the edge of the cornice with his hands.

He hesitated a moment, took a deep breath, and started to draw himself up. It was a difficult task, even for a man who always had been known as an athlete. He managed to get one elbow over the edge of the cornice, and thus he held himself, and rested, and tried to reduce his breathing to normal.

The hardest part of the task was before him, he knew. He had swung away from the window below. If he was forced to lower himself, he doubted whether he could swing his legs in enough to brace himself on the sill.

"Have to do it, now!" Roger Verbeck told himself.

Again he started drawing himself up. He got his other elbow over the edge of the cornice, rested again for an instant, and then started to turn. Now his chest rested against the cornice. He exerted all his strength and managed to get one leg up. It was not difficult, after that, to draw up the other. So he remained stretched on a narrow ledge twelve stories above a busy street, panting, almost exhausted, dizzy.

Verbeck closed his eyes and stretched himself out to his full length. He realized that he could not hope to go the remainder of the way until he had recovered his strength. However, it did not take him long to recuperate.

He raised himself on his elbows and glanced upward. The parapet was above him, and not difficult to scale, but to reach the edge of it he would have to stand up straight on the narrow ledge upon which he now was stretched.

Verbeck took a deep breath and started drawing up his knees. Presently he was in a kneeling position. Then, inch by inch, he raised his body. His hands crept up the face of the wall before him, stretched out and grasped the edge of the parapet.

Once more he was forced to draw himself up. He was very quiet about it, too. He did not know but that Landers might be directly above him, ready to receive him, or to thrust him over.

He got his elbows over the edge, and stopped to breathe and to listen. He could hear Kowen and Lawrence pounding on the door, and he found that Landers and the women were not near.

Verbeck began to think that good fortune was with him. He continued to draw himself up, and finally was stretched, panting, on the top of the parapet.

He was in no hurry, now. He had no intention of clashing physically with Landers while in an exhausted condition. There was no way, he thought, in which Landers and the women could escape from the roof except through the door at which the sheriff and Lawrence were pounding.

Verbeck waited until he felt refreshed, and then slipped down to the roof. Noiselessly he made his way across it toward the door. He came to a chimney, and stopped beside it, to watch and listen.

He had no weapon on him, and he knew that Landers had a vapor gun. One shot from that might render him unconscious, put him out of the fight. He could hear Landers and the women talking not very far from where he stood.

"They can't get through that door for some time," Landers was saying. "I'm going to telephone."

"He'll not come!" Mamie Blanchard wailed. "Why didn't we go down the stairs instead of up? We might have known we would have been caught in a trap."

"We'll see whether he'll come or not!" Landers said. "If the telephone is not out of commission—"

During the hot summer months, the roof was used as a garden. There was a little building in one corner of it that was used as a refreshment stand, and there always was a telephone there.

Verbeck knew that Landers was rushing across the roof to the building. He heard him smash against the frail door, heard it crash in. The women, it was evident, remained near the door leading to the stairs that went below.

Leaving the shadow of the chimney, Verbeck crept forward toward the little structure where Landers had gone to telephone. He hoped to catch the Black Star's lieutenant at a disadvantage and subdue him. He was much interested, too, in what Landers' telephone message might be, and to whom it would be sent.

Without a sound, Verbeck crossed the roof and came to the side of the little building. Landers had flashed an electric torch, and was taking the telephone from beneath the counter. Verbeck saw him take down the receiver.

CHAPTER XXIII

MUGGS GIVES A TIP

It was evident that the hotel switchboard operator was surprised to get a call from the roof.

"Oh, it's all right!" Verbeck heard Landers say. "I'm up on the roof with the Misses Whaley. One of the ladies is going to leave the city, and she wanted to call a friend from here—just a whim. I found the door unlocked."

Then he gave a number. Roger Verbeck made a mental note of it. Here might be a clew that would lead to something important.

Verbeck crept close to the door, and listened. Presently Landers spoke again.

"Hello! This is Landers! I'm trapped on the roof of the New Nortonia Hotel with Mamie and her sister. Kowen and his crowd are trying to break the door in now, but I think it'll take them some time, and then I can stand them off for a while. If you don't come for us, we're caught.... Yes, Verbeck and the sheriff. They walked in on us. I got them under control, but some others came. The place is a regular trap.... Thanks! But hurry!"

Verbeck slipped to one side as Landers put the receiver on the hook and hurried out. He followed the Black Star's lieutenant back across the roof, and watched as he met the women.

"He'll come for us!" Verbeck heard Landers say. "It'll take him some time, of course—fifteen minutes at least. We'll have to hold off those men on the other side of the door. If it comes to the worst, some of them will get something more than a dose out of a vapor gun. I don't intend to spend fifteen or twenty years in prison!"

"If we had only gone downstairs—" Mamie Blanchard

began.

"If we had, we'd have run into a few deputies. I tell you they planned to trap us! They've shadowed some of us—"

"Then it must have been you!" Mamie Blanchard told him. "I have not been out of the hotel, remember. It's your carelessness that got us into this mess!"

"Well, we won't quarrel about it," Landers said. "You women go to the other side of the roof and wait. I'll stay near the door and handle those men if they manage to break it open."

Landers approached the door, and Verbeck crept after him. The light was so faint that he could see little—just a shadow where the master crook's lieutenant was walking. Verbeck crouched as he advanced, made no noise, and was ready to stop if Landers betrayed any suspicion. But Landers, it appeared, did not expect a foe on the roof, and was intent only upon the door at which the sheriff and Lawrence were pounding.

Verbeck had picked up a piece of timber beside the little refreshment stand. It was the only weapon he had. He hated to use it, but he felt that the situation justified its use. Landers was about a match for him physically, and it was Verbeck's duty to make a prisoner of him, open the door, and let the others take the women into custody.

Landers was stamping upon the door.

"Get away, or I'll fire through it!" he called, as the pounding ceased for a moment.

He sent one shot crashing through the wood and Verbeck could hear a chorus of shrieks below. He knew Landers' plan—to delay them as much as he could. And for what? That was what Verbeck could not fathom.

To whom had Landers telephoned? How could he be rescued from the roof? Would the Black Star and his band face a battle with police and deputies, attempt to raid the hotel and save Landers and the two women?

Landers had stepped back, and was listening to what was

being said below. Verbeck crept forward until he was within six feet of the other man. He raised the piece of timber.

He sent but one blow home, but he knew as it struck that it would send Landers crashing to the roof, even though it did not render him unconscious. He sprang past him, and fumbled at the heavy bolts on the door, drew them, and threw the door open.

"Up—quick!" he cried.

Glad cries from the sheriff and Lawrence greeted him. They sprang to the roof, two deputies at their heels. They seized the groaning Landers, and rushed across the roof toward the women.

"Torches!" Kowen cried.

The torches flashed. The women were standing near one of the big chimneys. Kowen led his deputies toward them.

"You don't get away this time!" he said. "It's handcuffs and a cell for you! You've played your last game with the Black Star, you two beauties!"

The fair prisoners were led toward the stairs. Landers had been handcuffed, and was being carried to the floor below. Verbeck and Lawrence followed them, but when they reached the floor below, Verbeck called the sheriff aside.

"Landers telephoned from the refreshment stand on the roof," he said. "I have made a note of the number; it might lead us to something. But here is the funny part—he asked somebody to come and rescue him. How they are going to try it, I do not know; but I think that message went to the Black Star."

"Maybe he'll try a raid here," Kowen suggested.

"Landers estimated, so he told the women, that he would be here in fifteen minutes, at least. But how could even the Black Star get enough of his men together to raid a place like this in that length of time? It's the roof we have to watch. You remember how the Black Star escaped from the roof of the National Trust Building, don't you? He seems to have methods of which we know nothing."

"Some more of that light stuff, and talking to us out of the air, probably," the sheriff said. "Well, what shall we do?"

"Have your deputies put the prisoners in a room and guard them. We'll stay here by the door and watch the roof!"

Sheriff Kowen gave the orders. He and Verbeck remained by the door, Lawrence with them.

"What's the big idea?" Lawrence inquired.

"Perhaps nothing; we are waiting to see," Verbeck replied.

"Well, can't you let a fellow in on it? If it hadn't been for me, those people would be far away by this time; and you'd be bound and gagged in that room, waiting for the public to laugh at you!"

"Simply this," Verbeck said; "Landers telephoned to somebody to rescue him from the roof, and we are waiting to see who comes to do it, and how he comes."

They waited for ten minutes without hearing or seeing anything. They left the door and walked to the nearest chimney, and stood there, watching, listening, like men who expected something to drop from the sky.

And something did come from the sky—that puzzling, brilliant light they were learning to know so well. It flooded the roof, swept across it, almost blinding the three men there. Verbeck and Kowen and Lawrence ran back to the open door, shading their eyes with their hands.

The light disappeared and they heard the Black Star's voice. "What have you done with my people?" he shouted.

"We've put handcuffs on 'em, you crook!" Kowen shrieked. "And we'll do as much for you one of these days!"

"Watch out!" Verbeck warned.

Some sixth sense seemed to tell him what was coming. And it did—a vapor bomb that burst not ten feet from the doorway. They darted back and away from it. They saw the bright light flood the roof again. Then the darkness came once more, and they heard nothing more, saw nothing more.

"I'd like to know how he does that!" Kowen said. "Does he hang around in the sky like a star? Well, he didn't rescue anybody, anyway! That's one comfort!"

"He hasn't been more than fifteen minutes getting here," Verbeck said. "But we don't know how he is traveling, and so we can't judge how far away his headquarters might be. That telephone number—"

"We can investigate that, at any rate, the first thing in the morning," Kowen said. "I'll get the telephone people busy. Now I'll take these prisoners down to the jail and give each of them a nice little room, American plan."

The prisoners were taken away, the excitement in the hotel died down, Verbeck went to Lawrence's suite to smoke a cigarette and get away from the crowd for a time, and finally started home.

He was worrying about Muggs, for one thing. He was hoping that the valet would find some way in which he could be of service, while he was a prisoner in the Black Star's headquarters. He knew that Muggs could be depended upon to make every effort.

The Black Star's threat—about doing something sensational the following night—also came to his mind. Was the master rogue to win again? Was there no way in which he could be stopped, recaptured, put behind prison bars? Already the city was in the grip of terror. No man could tell where the Black Star would strike next. He might loot another bank, or a jewelry store, or raid the jail in an effort to rescue his companions in crime. The public was considering everything—except the thing that the Black Star had actually planned to do.

Mrs. Richard Branniton completed her arrangements for entertaining the distinguished diplomats, Lord Sambery and Sir Burton Banks, and had no thought that the master criminal might pay her residence a visit while her guests were enjoying themselves.

Verbeck reached his rooms and threw himself into an easy-chair to rest. He did not fear for himself. He did not think that the Black Star would make an attempt to abduct him again, for prisoners were only in the way at the master criminal's head-quarters. Also, there were half a dozen plain-clothes men in the apartment house, watching everybody who entered, ready to act in any emergency that might present itself.

It was too early to retire, so Verbeck smoked, and tried to read a magazine, but found that he could not get himself inter-ested. He disliked to go to one of his clubs, for all the other members would want to discuss the Black Star and nothing else.

He started across the room to get a favorite book from the case, but whirled around and went back, because the telephone had rung.

"Hello!" he called.

"Verbeck?"

"Yes."

"This is the Black Star. Some of my men have informed me how Landers and the two women were caught. It took courage to climb to the roof the way you did, but that is not the point. Those three people are very necessary members of my organi-zation, and I want them released."

Verbeck laughed into the telephone.

"Have you called the sheriff?" he asked. "He seems to be the man in charge just now."

"I have not called the sheriff yet. I thought I'd call you first, and get you to influence him. You see, Verbeck, I have Muggs here with me."

"What has that to do with it?"

"Simply this—if I have to descend to violence, I'll do it. Nothing shall stop me from having my revenge upon the city. Unless those people of mine are released by noon tomorrow, I'll blow the jail off the map—and I'll attend to Mr. Muggs."

"In what way?" Verbeck asked.

"I'll simply have him knocked on the head and dumped into the river. If I have to be violent, I'll be a proper thug! What have you to say?"

"Nothing, except that you have a wonderful nerve to speak as you do."

"Perhaps you think I can't blow the jail to pieces?"

"I do not say you can't, but I don't think you'll do it—not with Landers and The Princess inside it."

"And maybe you think I'd hesitate about making away with Muggs, do you?"

"I scarcely think you'll do anything of the sort," Verbeck said. "You would accomplish nothing, and you'd be hanged for murder after we caught you."

"You don't think I am serious," the Black Star replied. "I agreed to give you until noon tomorrow—"

"But I couldn't make the sheriff turn them loose! You may be sure that he'll guard them well, and see that they stand trial. Why, if they were turned loose—"

"I'll arrange that. They are to be freed and put in the middle of the polo field. I'll do the rest. On second thought, I'll give you more time, Verbeck, if you have to argue with the sheriff. I'm going to be busy tomorrow night, as I have said. I'll give you until the following morning. I'll ring you up then for your answer; and it had better be what I want to hear."

"You actually think we'd do such a thing?" Verbeck asked. "We'd look pretty, wouldn't we, turning three criminals loose because another criminal asked it!"

"Not an ordinary criminal—but the Black Star! And I don't ask it—I demand it! Muggs is here, and I am going to let him speak to you. Perhaps you don't really believe that he is here. He'll tell you that I am serious and mean what I say."

Verbeck waited, his heart pounding at his ribs. If Muggs only had the presence of mind, if he—

"Hello, boss!" came Muggs' voice over the wire.

"Hello, Muggs."

"I'm sure here in this big crook's headquarters, boss. I don't know what he intends to hand me, but it'll be plenty."

"Muggs, what do you want me to do?" Verbeck asked.

"Well, maybe I'm prejudiced," Muggs said, "but I don't care to be knocked on the head and thrown in any river. It wouldn't be a hard job for them—the river ain't far away!" That was a hint, at least. "And it ain't exactly nice to be croaked with music ringin' in your ears—"

Verbeck heard an exclamation of rage, the sound of a blow, a gasp, and then nothing more except a little click that told him the wire was dead. Muggs had tried to give a tip, and had not been given a chance to complete it.

CHAPTER XXIV

ON THE TRAIL

Verbeck tried to remember the exact words that Muggs had spoken. He had said plainly that the headquarters of the Black Star were not far from the river. That in itself was a help, but not a very great one.

There were thousands of places in the city, not far from the river, where the Black Star could hide and where the members of his band could visit him. The headquarters might be in a warehouse on the water front, in some pretentious mansion on the hills overlooking the stream.

And what else was it that Muggs had said? That he didn't want to die with music ringing in his ears! Verbeck wondered what that might mean, for it was the statement, evidently, that had caused such a quick end to the conversation.

Verbeck paced the floor and thought it out. He knew the city from one end to the other. He had been born there, reared there, had watched it grow. Music ringing in his ears—

"The resort park!" Verbeck gasped. "That's what he must have meant! The Black Star's headquarters will be found near the river and near the resort park, where the band plays every afternoon and evening!"

Verbeck rushed to the telephone, called the sheriff, and asked him to come to his apartment immediately.

"I've got a tip that's better than the last one," he said. "Muggs gave it to me."

"Muggs?"

"Don't ask me to explain now. Hurry up here. And have the telephone people investigate that number I gave you, and report to you here about it."

Then Verbeck called the chief of police, finally locating him at his home.

"Chief, there's no use keeping up the bluff any longer," he said. "The Black Star knows very well that I am still after him. I wish you'd get over to my apartment as soon as you can. I've got something important to tell you. Kowen will be here—"

"Why did you call Kowen?" the chief demanded. "Couldn't we handle it alone? I understand Kowen won enough glory tonight to last him a month."

"Come over, and do your quarreling here!" Verbeck said.

Kowen was the first to arrive, fifteen minutes later.

"What's the big tip?" he asked. "Anything to it?"

"Wait until the chief gets here."

"Did you send for the chief? Was that necessary, Verbeck? It seems to me that we worked pretty well together this evening. Why give the police some of the credit? I lost the Black Star, remember, and I ought to have a chance to get him back!"

"There'll be work enough for all of us—and glory enough," Verbeck assured him.

Then the chief came storming in and exchanged glares with the sheriff.

"Before we begin, it might be well to have an understanding," Verbeck said. "You gentlemen must stop scrapping and become allies. We have a big job on hand, and we want to wind it up as quickly as possible."

Then he told them of his conversation with the Black Star, and of what Muggs had said.

"Let them go?" Kowen screeched. "I'd let him wreck the town first! Those crooks are in jail, and they're going to stay there!"

"That isn't the point," Verbeck interrupted. "It's the little tip Muggs gave that interests us. According to what he said, the Black Star's headquarters are near the river, and I believe, when he spoke of the music, that he meant the resort park."

"I think you're right!" the chief exclaimed.

"But where could the headquarters be in that locality?" the sheriff wanted to know.

"It's our job to find out," the chief said, "and we'll start at daylight. If we can locate it before night, perhaps we can stop whatever it is that the big crook intends to do."

The telephone bell rang again. The call was for the sheriff, and he spent some time listening to the person at the other end of the wire. When he turned toward them again, his face was beaming.

"It begins to look good," he said. "That was from the manager of the telephone company. He looked up that number that Landers called. It is a little summer cottage far up the river beyond the resort park."

"Great!" the chief exclaimed. "We'll land 'em yet!"

"But that isn't the funny thing about it. The manager says he sent a man out there in a machine. There is nobody living in the cottage, and there hasn't been for months, yet the telephone bills have been paid regularly."

"Meaning," said Verbeck, "that the bills are paid by one of the Black Star's organization. Of course his headquarters are not in the cottage. But we'll find the place somewhere in that locality."

"Where do you get that?" Kowen asked.

"It means simply that somewhere between the cottage and the next station on the line, the Black Star has plugged in on the wire. When that number is called, the bell rings in his own headquarters. When he calls, it appears to the switchboard operator that the number is calling."

"I believe you've got it!" the chief cried.

"In the morning, you can go to that cottage and follow the wire, examine every foot of it, discover where the other wire is plugged in, follow it, and find the place that we want. Other men can search through the neighborhood. We're on the right track!"

For another hour they worked perfecting their plans, and then the chief and the sheriff, friendly again, took their departure. Verbeck left a call at the office for an early hour, and made haste to retire and fortify himself with sleep.

He was up soon after break of day, had his bath and breakfast, and went down to get his roadster from the garage, feeling particularly fit. He drove immediately to police headquarters and went into the private office of the chief, who with Sheriff Kowen was waiting for him.

"I had twenty men out there at daybreak working on that telephone line," the chief said. "They are scattered, of course— look like linemen. In fact, they are making a bluff at stringing a new line—but they are searching for the place where the Black Star taps the wire. It wouldn't surprise me much to find that the Black Star knows as much about our plans as we know ourselves—he seems to be able to get all the information he wants—but maybe we can get the better of the fiend this time!"

"Are we going to wait here for that wire squad to report?" Kowen asked.

"No; there is no use in that," the chief replied. "I have sent twenty more men out there—all in plain clothes. They went out a couple at a time; have been going out since midnight. Some are near the resort park and others are scattered through the woods. Did you send your deputies to the other side, sheriff?"

"I did; between us we have men on the north, east and south, and the river is on the west. Maybe we have that crook's headquarters surrounded, and maybe we haven't."

"We may as well start out there," Verbeck put in.

The chief got into the roadster with him; the sheriff had a car of his own, driven by a deputy. They drove rapidly through the city and out along the river road. They came to the resort, and got out and parked their cars. The sheriff and the chief began receiving reports from their forces.

All the buildings in the resort had been searched well, and nothing found. Men had discovered nothing suspicious in the woods. There was a large fish cannery near, and it had been investigated thoroughly. The men scattered around the woods were closing in, drawing the net tighter.

The wire squad was at work. They had followed the wire from the little cottage, after making an investigation there and being sure that the cottage was not the entrance to a subterranean abode used by the Black Star. Even while the man in charge of the squad was making his report, word was flashed down the line that the extra wire had been found.

The sheriff and chief got into Verbeck's machine, and he drove them a quarter of a mile down the road. The wire had been tapped in a very clever manner, as one of the electricians of the department explained. It was running underground, through a small cable.

The chief called for more of his men, and they began unearthing the line. It seemed to run straight toward the east, and through the woods. The chief sent a captain and half a dozen men ahead of the wire squad.

"We're getting close to them, I think," the chief declared. "I feel that this is going to be our lucky day."

After a time they found a telephone instrument attached to the wire and hidden beneath a heap of brush. Next they came upon the old farmhouse, with the wire fence around it. There the telephone wire left the ground and ran from tree to tree through the grove, to disappear into the building.

"There!" the chief said. "We'll get the place surrounded—"

He gave quick orders, and the force of officers began closing in. Within a few minutes, the house had a circle of determined men around it. Verbeck and the chief had been watching it closely, while the sheriff placed the men. They had seen no sign of life.

"Probably gone—if this is really the place," Verbeck said. "It wouldn't have been difficult for the Black Star to learn our plans, and he had all night in which to get away."

"Well, we'll get in there, anyway," the chief said. "It may be our luck that he is still there with some of his gang. If he is gone, and had to get out in a hurry, he might have left something behind that will give us a clew as to what he intends doing tonight."

"And we could put a lot of trust in that, couldn't we?" said Roger Verbeck. "He won over us before, because we gave considerable attention to some bogus orders he left on a table in a bogus headquarters—don't forget that."

"I'm not liable to; the precious newspapers won't let me," said the chief.

The men were creeping through the brush now, approaching the fence. Verbeck had the chief issue an order for them to stop.

"I don't like the looks of that fence," he said. "You'll notice that the house is old and weather-beaten, and about to fall to pieces, from its appearance; but the fence is a substantial one, and new. I have an idea that the man who touches that fence will meet with serious trouble."

"By George, it is a new fence!" the chief admitted.

"Wait!" Verbeck said.

He crawled forward alone, foot by foot, stopping now and then to glance toward the old farmhouse, and made his way toward the fence that held the deadly current.

CHAPTER XXV

END OF THE TRAIL

Half a dozen feet from the fence Verbeck stopped. He watched the house for a couple of minutes, and then advanced another pace. He was within three feet of the fence now, and he saw what he had expected—wires and cables of metal cunningly woven in the mesh of the structure itself, and in such manner that the whole thing would be charged when a current was turned on.

The chief had crawled up behind Verbeck.

"That fence is deadly!" Verbeck said. "The Black Star used something like this once before, you'll remember, and half a dozen men were seriously shocked and burned. We don't dare try to pass it at present. The current may or may not be running through it. We can't take the chance. If the gate was open, we probably could pass through without danger, but the gate is a part of the circuit."

"Well, are we going to let a fence tie us up?" the chief asked. "If the Black Star and his band are inside, every minute we spend out here gives them a chance to get ready for us."

"Warn the men!" Verbeck said.

The chief sent the word around the circle of officers—nobody was to touch the fence, since it probably was charged with a deadly current, and shocks and burns would result. Sheriff Kowen had crawled up to them through the brush.

"Look!" he exclaimed suddenly.

A dog, attracted by the men in the woods, had been running from one group to another. Now, chasing a stick one of the men had thrown, he brushed against the fence. A single yelp came from him; and he was stretched on the ground, apparently lifeless.

"You see?" Verbeck said. "Perhaps it wouldn't kill a man, but it would burn him badly, and put him out of the game."

"We've got to get through!" the chief declared. "And how are we going to do it?"

One of the electricians had crawled forward, and they explained the situation to him.

"If the current is that strong, we can't fool with it," he said earnestly. "Electricity isn't a timid plaything at best, and a dose like that fence hands out is too much for anybody. You'll notice that the dog hasn't moved; he's dead. And since we can't get through that fence—"

"We can go over it!" Verbeck added.

"How?" the chief and sheriff asked in chorus.

"Bridge the thing," said Verbeck. "We've got men enough, and there are trees enough."

"It'll be one ticklish job," the electrician warned.

"But it can be done," Verbeck declared. "Chief, have all your men watch the house closely. If anybody in there tries to interfere with me, bombard the place."

Verbeck sprang up and ran parallel to the fence for a distance of half a hundred feet. He had spotted a big tree there that had a projecting branch not fifteen feet from the ground—a branch half a foot in diameter that extended over the fence and into the yard about the house. He swung himself into the tree, reached the branch, and crept out along it. He crossed over the deadly fence, hesitated a moment, and dropped. Roger Verbeck was inside.

He found that he was partially screened from the house by a clump of brush. He turned his back upon the house and crept toward the fence again. The chief and sheriff hurried to meet him.

"Almost all your men can do as I have done," Verbeck said. "We don't even have to bridge it. Have them come over, one by one, and have the others watch the house closely. If the Black Star or any of his men are in there, they know we are after them and are watching us."

The chief issued the orders. The men made the perilous trip one at a time, and dropped to the ground beside Verbeck. Twenty men in all crossed over, and left the others to guard outside the fence, maintaining the blockade around the house.

Not a sign had come from within to show that their presence was known. But Verbeck and those who had fought against the Black Star before knew that that did not mean safety. It was like the Black Star to wait for the proper moment before striking.

"Be careful, you men!" Verbeck warned. "We are fighting the Black Star, please remember, and he can be unscrupulous at times. You may consider yourselves in danger from the moment we start toward the house. In his old headquarters he had some of the most diabolical traps known to man; and you always find them where you least expect them. Beware of the doors and windows. Investigate them before you touch them; and if we get inside the place, be alert continually. You may expect pitfalls, vapor bombs—anything!"

The officers scattered and surrounded the house inside the fence. Those on the outside crept as close as they dared, weapons held ready, and watched the doors and windows.

On and on went those inside the fence, until they were almost against the walls. The chief, the sheriff, and Verbeck were at the front.

"Doesn't seem to be anybody around," the chief said. "They got wise and left, I suppose. Well, we'll investigate the place anyway, since we are here."

He started up the steps that led to the small veranda at the front of the house. His foot struck the lowest step.

There was a sharp explosion, and half the veranda was torn away. Verbeck and the others reeled backward. A cloud of smoke filled the air; and it was not the pungent vapor used by the Black Star in his bombs.

"That was the real thing!" Verbeck declared.

The chief was pale and trembling as he retreated.

"I'll get that fiend!" he declared. "Look at the hole that explosion made in the porch floor! If a man had been over that—"

"They set it off too quick!" the sheriff said. "We've got to move carefully, or we'll be having casualties."

"We must take that chance!" the chief said. "We've got to get that fiend, and policemen are paid to run into trouble when it is necessary. Into the house, men! Get in any way that you can! Try to take care of yourselves, but get in!"

The officers cheered and shouted. They plunged toward windows and doors. They smashed panes of glass in, and hurled themselves against doors as if they knew no fear.

Half a dozen explosions came, but no man was injured. Here and there a policeman made an entrance, and others followed him. Within five minutes Verbeck and the chief and Kowen found that all were inside, gathered in the big hall at the front of the house, and that no man had received a scratch.

"I guess we're on the right trail, sure enough!" the chief said.

"And this is where we must be careful," declared Roger Verbeck. "This is where we are liable to run into traps."

The search of the house began. There were but two floors and the basement, and the search started at the top. There the officers found nothing except unoccupied rooms that were filled with dust. They even went into the garret, and found nothing except a heap of discarded clothing that looked as if it had been there for years.

Next they searched the ground floor. In the rear was a kitchen, almost immaculate, with its pots and pans and stores of food. There were three bed-chambers that appeared to be in constant use. And that was all.

"I suppose it is in the basement, as usual," Verbeck said.

"Careful, men!" the chief warned. "If they are in the basement, they'll put up a fight. That big crook knows what is in store for him when he's caught, so you don't want to bank too much on that old bunk of his that he abhors violence. A cornered rat will put up a stiff fight!"

They found the basement door. Roger Verbeck went forward, grasped the knob, and jerked the door open suddenly. Again there was a rending explosion, and the panels and framework were shattered. Back through the hall staggered Verbeck and the others. The vapor the master crook used was mingled with the smoke of the explosion, and was sweeping through the hall.

But the police had been prepared for it. They ran to the open windows and inhaled the fresh air, remaining there until the poisonous fumes had been swept out of the open front door. Then they rushed back into the hall.

Before them was a stairway shrouded in dense darkness. Verbeck took an electric torch in one hand and his automatic in the other, and began the descent, a detective immediately behind him. He flashed the torch on the stairs, hesitated before treading upon each one, made his way step by step toward the bottom, expecting every instant to hear the crash of another explosion.

He reached the end of the flight, and found himself in a narrow hall. Along this he went, a file of other men behind him. He came to a door.

"This seems to be the place," he whispered. "If they are inside, we are due for a warm reception."

He grasped the handle and jerked the door open. This time there was no explosion. He flashed his torch again. In front of the door was a heavy curtain of some sort.

Verbeck put out his hand and moved the curtain aside gently. He could see into the room—could see in the path of the electric torch, and that was all.

Verbeck knew that the situation was precarious. It meant something to enter a dark room in which the Black Star and some of his men might be waiting. It took courage, the more so since Roger Verbeck was well acquainted with the master rogue's methods, and realized that the Black Star was fighting for freedom now.

"Hold the curtain—and wait!" Verbeck whispered to the man nearest him.

He slipped inside the curtain and stood with his back against it. He had extinguished the torch. There was not a glimmer of light, not the slightest sound.

Verbeck held his automatic ready, and suddenly flashed the torch in his left hand. He played it down the length of the room, sweeping the streak of light from side to side.

"In!" he cried to the others. "Torches!"

They crowded into the room, their lights flashing. The room was thoroughly illuminated. The chief gave a cry that was echoed by the sheriff and the others.

Without a doubt, they were in the Black Star's headquarters. Verbeck knew the room instantly for the one in which he had been prisoner for a short time. There were the long table, the blackboards, and on the table a black robe and mask that had been discarded by some member of the band.

"Careful!" the chief warned.

"I don't think there is any need of caution," said Roger Verbeck. "I have an idea that neither the Black Star nor any of his people are around the place. He knew we had got on the right trail—and he has moved. The Black Star always has another headquarters prepared, remember. He moved half a dozen times the last time we fought against him. There is a lamp on the table—one of you men light it."

Verbeck walked across the room to the blackboard, upon

which there was some fine writing.

"I thought so!" he exclaimed.

This is what he read:

> Gentlemen: I am aware that you are going to locate the place where I live and work, and so I suppose I am forced to move. Had not that fool of a Landers telephoned me from the roof of the hotel, had not Roger Verbeck overheard the number he called, I would have been safe here as long as I wished to remain.
>
> I am leaving for a new place that already has been prepared for me. I am taking Muggs along as a sort of hostage. There is no rush, since I have all night to make the move.
>
> When I go, I shall leave bombs attached to some of the windows and doors, and connected with the veranda steps. They will annoy you, perhaps, and make you think that you are brave men rushing into danger. It is just a little joke.
>
> For this inconvenience, the city shall be made to pay dearly, of course. It costs me something each time I move my headquarters. I have to leave furniture behind, and I have to inform all my people of the new location. But the people of the city shall pay! Tonight, I strike, and I shall strike hard!

"Fooled again!" the chief shrieked, in rage. "And we were on the right trail, too!"

"We'll get him yet!" declared Sheriff Kowen. "Some of his people will make another slip—"

"And, in the meantime," Roger Verbeck interrupted, "we'd better be preparing for tonight and what it may bring forth. After this, the Black Star will strike with twice his usual strength and cunning. He has said he would—and the crook always keeps his word!"

CHAPTER XXVI

THE BIG BLOW

Reduced to a state of unconsciousness by means of a vapor gun, Muggs was moved, some time during the night, to the new headquarters. When he regained consciousness he found himself in a room similar to the old one, except that it was somewhat smaller. Muggs did not know in what section of the city he was.

The Black Star was speaking over the telephone, and as Muggs sat up on the couch, he hung up the receiver and turned around.

"Well, Muggs, we have had a bit of excitement," the master crook said. "Verbeck risked his life to get to the roof of a certain hotel, but he managed to get a telephone number that caused us considerable trouble. I have just received a report from one of my men. He tells me that Verbeck, and a squad of police and deputies, have surrounded the old house and are creeping upon it as if it contained a crowd of desperate characters. They will have some excitement, too, Muggs, and then will discover nothing but an empty nest."

"Yeh?" Muggs asked. "They'll discover you, too, one of these days; and then I hope they give you life!"

"Inclined toward violence again, Muggs, when I have been treating you so nicely? I am really ashamed of you."

"As if I cared!" Muggs scoffed.

"I am thinking of taking you along tonight, Muggs, when we call upon Mrs. Richard Branniton and her guests. But if you are not a good boy, I shall leave you at home."

The Black Star chuckled and turned toward the end of the table. The bell on the wall tinkled, and a robed and masked man entered and went to the blackboard, which here was installed on one side of the room.

"Number Three," he wrote.

"Countersign?"

"Colorado."

"Report," wrote the Black Star.

"Lord Sambery and Sir Burton Banks arrived on time and now are at the Branniton house."

"Any new developments?"

"None have been learned. We are watching closely," wrote Number Three.

"I have decided to seize Branniton himself tonight, with the other two, and hold him for ransom," the Black Star wrote. "You will have your squad attend to it, and be sure that they do not fail. The man who prosecuted me must be punished."

"I shall attend to it, and warn the men that they must not fail."

"There have been no changes in transportation means?"

"None whatever."

"That is all. Retire," the Black Star wrote.

The man backed through the door and closed it after him.

"You're goin' to run against a snag," Muggs told the Black Star. "You're bitin' off more than you can chew, and it's likely to choke you!"

"I scarcely think so, Muggs. This little affair is so well planned that there can be no failure. It is the master stroke of my career. It will add to my fame, and, at the same time, it will be highly profitable. When the news gets out, the country will be shocked."

"You go to monkeyin' with the government, and you'll get yours!" Muggs told him again. "Them gents are guests of the government, ain't they?"

"I should think that they were, Muggs. They are here on very important international business. I may mention that it is so important that I expect to collect the ransom within forty-eight hours. I understand there are certain negotiations pending, and that there can be no delay."

The Black Star sat down at the end of the table and began consulting his memorandum book again, completely ignoring Muggs, who remained sitting on the couch. Muggs' hands were lashed together, and he knew that he was being watched continually. And yet he felt that he had a duty to perform.

"I ain't helpin' the boss at all," Muggs mused. "I tried to, once, and I fell down. If this big crook puts that over tonight, it'll make the boss a bigger laughingstock than before. Gee, I wish I could do somethin'!"

Verbeck was wishing the same thing late that afternoon. When it came to locating the new headquarters of the master crook, the police and deputies admitted that they did not know which way to turn.

Meanwhile the city was in terror. The Black Star had said that he would strike tonight—and strike hard. Banks and financial institutions were sending in frantic demands that they be given adequate police protection. Jewelry establishments were doing the same. Private detective agencies were swamped with orders for operatives. From one end of the city to the other, men and women asked the question, where would the Black Star strike?

Mrs. Richard Branniton was not thinking of the master rogue. She was busy entertaining her distinguished guests. Luncheon had been served, and they were being shown the city. Then they returned to the Branniton residence, and sought their suites to get some rest before the reception of the evening.

Branniton had engaged four more private detectives, making eight in all, and had planned to have them scattered about the house. But that was the ordinary safeguard against ordinary jewel thieves, and had nothing to do with the Black Star. Branniton was not thinking of the master crook, either. His mind was upon the fact that he was gathering political influence by entertaining the two famous diplomats.

Late that afternoon, Roger Verbeck went to police headquarters for a conference with the chief and Sheriff Kowen.

"We can't do anything except have our men waiting and ready," the chief said. "I've received about a thousand reports from my men, and there isn't one of them worth the paper it's written on. They seem to think they've got to report something or get into trouble with me. The papers are right—the police are a gang of fools and court jesters!"

"Well, what can we do?" Kowen complained. "Did we get credit for getting on that crook's trail? We did not. The evening papers are roasting us because we didn't nab him. I'm getting pretty sick of this business!"

"We wouldn't be in this business if you hadn't been asleep and let that gang get the Black Star out of jail!" the chief reminded him.

"Wait!" Verbeck commanded. "Are we going to fight among ourselves? Is that a way to catch the Black Star?"

"What's the matter with Muggs?" the chief demanded.

"The chances are that Muggs is not able to do anything," Verbeck replied. "I can imagine that he is being watched closely since he gave me that little tip over the telephone; and I'm hoping that nothing worse has happened to him. Muggs, you may be sure, will help us if he gets the chance."

Nightfall found them still at police headquarters. They had sent out for something to eat. The police reserves had been gathered. Kowen had his deputies ready. The Black Star, they knew, might strike at eight in the evening, at midnight, at three in the morning. They had to be ready. Their one hope was to get a quick alarm, to reach the scene in time to capture the master rogue, or at least important members of his band.

The residence of Richard Branniton was a blaze of light. Guests were arriving—prominent men, beautiful women, bejeweled leaders of the city's society. An orchestra was playing in the ballroom. Men and women were greeting one another, laughing and chatting.

The Branniton residence was surrounded by wide lawns studded with big maple trees. Here and there were dark spaces not reached by the lights from either the house or the street. Two blocks away was a small park.

At nine thirty o'clock several men approached this park singly, each acting as if he was going about his business or hurrying to his home. They followed the walks, and now and then they passed and whispered a few words to one another.

More men happened to walk through the alley in the rear of the Branniton house. Some of these men had bundles beneath their arms. There was a door in the alley wall, and before it was a caterer's wagon. Men were carrying refreshments into the house.

At one of the corners of the residence, in the rear, there was a small veranda that was shrouded in darkness. While the caterer's men were carrying in the provisions, several of the other men, who had been in the alley, slipped through the door and sought the dark veranda. Crouched there, they waited.

Here and there a shadow flitted across the lawn from dark spot to dark spot—but the shadows were men. A big limousine stopped on a side street half a block away, the shades drawn at all its windows. A truck stalled on the other side street, apparently, and four men in it worked at the engine. Finally one left, saying he would telephone for help.

Across the avenue from the Branniton residence a crowd had gathered to watch the guests arrive, muttering when two police officers urged them to move on. In the crowd were several men who gave one another knowing looks now and then.

The last guests arrived. The hour of ten struck. Inside the Branniton house the orchestra was playing and couples were dancing. Mrs. Richard Branniton was beaming upon her guests, and her husband was seeking to make an impression upon Sir

Burton Banks and Lord Sambery. Branniton had hopes of receiving an important diplomatic post abroad.

As the hour of ten struck, the men beside the dark rear veranda unfastened the bundles they had been carrying, and put on black robes and masks. More men approached the house from the other side, keeping in the shadows, and when they reached the darkness near the wall put on robes and masks.

At ten minutes after the hour of ten, thirty men had gathered beside the dark veranda, and fifteen more were scattered near the house, on guard. In the midst of these thirty men, the Black Star suddenly appeared.

"I want no mistakes!" he whispered. "Is every man in his proper place?"

"Yes, sir," one of them replied.

"One of the waiters is a man of ours. Has he reported?"

"Not yet, sir."

They waited a few minutes, and another man slipped around the corner of the house.

"Everything is ready, sir," he reported. He was the waiter.

"How soon can you do your part?" the Black Star asked.

"In about five minutes."

"Off for about three minutes, and then on again!"

"Yes, sir," said the waiter, and he slipped away and reëntered the house.

The Black Star whispered a command, and the men scattered, keeping well in the darkness, but gradually surrounding the house, except in front, where it was brilliantly lighted.

And suddenly the lights in the house went out!

Feminine shrieks, boisterous laughter, jests came from those within. To them it was a joke—a fuse burned out at a critical time. Branniton called upon his servants to ascertain the cause of the trouble immediately and remedy it.

Then, as suddenly as they had been extinguished, the lights came on again. The waiter had manipulated the switch in the basement as the Black Star had instructed.

Mrs. Richard Branniton's guests shrieked in alarm now. The doors had been closed; the shades had been drawn at the windows. And before each door and window stood a man dressed in a black robe, with a black mask over his face. Each one so dressed held a weapon menacingly before him.

A voice from the hallway caused them to turn. They saw a tall man dressed in a robe, his face covered with a mask—and on the hood of his robe was a flaming star of jet.

"Do not make a move, ladies and gentlemen!" he cried. "I am the Black Star, and these are my men! We will use violence if we are forced to do so, though we'd rather not. I may mention that the few detectives you had in the house have been taken care of, and you are absolutely at our mercy. The telephone wires are cut, too. We are here to make a collection of rare jewels and ornaments, and to carry away with us three men."

"You crook!" Branniton cried, rushing toward him.

The Black Star raised his arm. A vapor gun exploded. Richard Branniton crashed to the floor. Women screamed.

"He is not injured—merely rendered unconscious!" the Black Star called out. "If you faint, ladies, I am afraid that nobody will be able to take care of you, so please don't do it. Line up against that wall, ladies—and the gentlemen against this one. Remember—my men will fire at the first move any of you make!"

CHAPTER XXVII

MUGGS TAKES A CHANCE

It was an evening of varied experiences for Muggs, one that he liked to remember later as being the acme in adventure and chance taking.

Muggs had been held a prisoner in the headquarters room at the place to which he had been moved, listening to the Black Star perfect his arrangements for his descent upon the Branniton residence—a prisoner who was allowed to see and to hear, yet was helpless to give a warning.

Now and then he got up from the couch and walked back and forth across the room, while the master criminal chuckled behind his mask, and frequently indulged his taste for sarcastic remarks.

"My dear Muggs, it would be a feather in your cap, would it not, if you were able to tell the authorities all that you know now?" the Black Star asked. "What a sensation you could cause by walking into police headquarters and shrieking your information into the ears of the chief and the sheriff and Roger Verbeck! But I am afraid that you will not be able to do anything of the sort, Muggs. However, we all have our little disappointments in life."

"You'll have somethin' worse than a disappointment before this thing is over!" Muggs snarled.

"You are still inclined toward violence—eh, Muggs? You should cultivate a more peaceful nature, such as I possess. Violence merely destroys itself, my dear Muggs."

"Yeh, and I'll probably destroy you before we make an end of this!" Muggs declared. "I tell you that you can't get away with it! You're about due to strangle on what you've bitten off!"

The Black Star did not reply to that; he merely chuckled and went back to the end of the table to consult his memorandum book again. It appeared to Muggs that the master crook consulted that book to a great extent this day, acting as if he felt that there was some minor detail he had forgotten.

After a time, the little bell on the wall tinkled, and a robed and masked figure entered the room and went to the blackboard. Muggs glanced at him in disgust. The Black Star's men had been reporting continually during the day.

"Number Five," the man wrote.

"Countersign?" wrote the Black Star on his blackboard.

"Everglades."

"Report."

"There appears to be no suspicion as to what we really intend to do tonight. The police reserves are being held in waiting, and the sheriff has his deputies ready for action, but those seem to be all the arrangements that have been made."

"How about Verbeck?" the Black Star wrote.

"He is at police headquarters now, waiting for the alarm so he can take the trail."

"Good. That is all," the Black Star wrote.

The member of the band bowed and backed through the door. The Black Star wrote something in the memorandum book, closed it and put it into a drawer in the table. Then he turned toward Muggs again.

"Muggs, I have decided to have you remain here this evening," he said, "I cannot spare the time to watch you, and so shall not take you with me."

"Thanks for that much!" Muggs growled.

"You will remain in this room, Muggs, and I shall have to keep your wrists lashed together, of course. I know that it will be uncomfortable—but that is the penalty for discovering my old headquarters and forcing us to move. I can't have you interfering with my plans tonight, you know."

"If I had a chance, I'd interfere with 'em, all right!"

"But the chance is missing—eh, Muggs? Do you mean you'd try to prevent me from making a fortune for my band by running away with some jewels and a couple of diplomats?"

"You haven't run away with them yet," Muggs told him.

"It is only a matter of an hour or so, my dear Muggs. Probably I shall bring those diplomats here. You'll have the chance, Muggs, to associate with a lord and a knight."

The Black Star rang, and his servant entered.

"I am going to leave our prisoner here tonight when I leave," the Black Star said. "I expect to find him here when I return. You understand?"

"He'll be here, sir!" the servant promised.

"As long as he behaves himself, give him the liberty of this room," the master criminal went on to say. "If he does not behave, handle him in your own way."

"Yes, sir."

"Tell the mechanic to be ready to start in ten minutes."

The servant hurried out. The Black Star glanced into his memorandum book again, and paced the floor, now and then looking at the little clock on the table. After a time, the servant returned.

"The mechanic is ready, sir," he reported.

"Good. Take care of Muggs while I am gone, but do not pester him so long as he is a good boy."

"He'd better not pester me!" Muggs growled.

The Black Star wrapped his robe closely around him, and put on the heavy ulster over it. He looked at Muggs once more, his eyes glittering through the mask. Then he chuckled, and hurried through the door.

Muggs threw himself full length on the couch and glared at the man who acted as the master rogue's servant.

"I'm gettin' mighty tired of this," he complained. "The eats are all right, and I suppose I hadn't ought to kick, but it ain't nice to have your wrists tied together all the time."

"If you're schemin' to get me to unfasten 'em, you ain't goin' to work the scheme, I can tell you that!" the servant declared. "Them wrists of yours stay just as they are, far as I'm concerned."

"You'd better never let me get 'em loose!" Muggs warned him.

"You wouldn't do much if they were."

"Is that so? I could separate you into sections in about ten minutes!" Muggs told him.

The servant laughed, sat down at the end of the table, and started to smoke. Muggs glared at him, rolled over, and turned his back to the room and the man in it.

Muggs might not have shown it outwardly, but he was almost frantic. The Black Star and his men were on their way, he knew. Before long they would surround the Branniton residence. They would get inside, rob women guests of their jewels, kidnap the two diplomats and Branniton, and rush away again before the police could reach the scene. Once more the public would howl, and the newspapers would ask why the police and Roger Verbeck did not capture the master criminal who did much as he pleased with the wealth of the town.

Muggs did not know, of course, where he was at the present moment. This new headquarters might be out at the edge of the city, or in the very heart of it. But Muggs did know that, if he could escape from the building, there would be a chance of warning the police and Verbeck, possibly in time for them to do something.

He tested the cords that lashed his wrists, and told himself for the hundredth time that they could not be removed. Everything had been taken from his pockets, including his knife. He had glanced around the headquarters room whenever he had a chance, and he had failed to see anything that might help him.

To get his wrists free—that was the first task. And then he

would have to escape from the place, wherever it was. He did not know whether the servant was the only man remaining there; the Black Star might have others around, on guard. Nor were men all that had to be considered. There might be traps in the house, there might be another deadly fence, or something like that.

Muggs was beginning to feel desperate. He knew that every second had its value now. He rolled over, sat up on the couch, and yawned.

"I sure hope the Black Star turns me loose tomorrow," he said. "He hinted that he might, after he pulled off tonight's stunt."

"Yes, and maybe he won't, unless the sheriff lets Landers and those two women go," the servant said.

"Gee, the sheriff won't do that. Even my boss couldn't make him do it. He's got those three in the jug, and there they'll stay, unless the Black Star rescues them himself." Muggs got up and walked slowly to the table. "There ain't any law against me havin' a smoke, is there?" he asked.

"Help yourself—anything like that goes as long as you behave," the servant replied.

"The Black Star has a good brand of cigarettes, I'll say that much for him," said Muggs. "My boss smokes the same kind."

"You're kinder crazy about that boss of yours, ain't you?" the servant asked.

"Sure! Why not? He saved my life, and he certainly has helped me since. He gives me a steady job, good money, and treats me decent."

"He ain't like the general run of bosses, then."

"I should say not!" Muggs declared.

He put a cigarette in his mouth and picked up a match. It was an awkward task with his bound wrists. He struck the match, held the flame to the end of the cigarette, and puffed a cloud of smoke.

"If every man had a boss like mine," Muggs continued, "the world would be a better place. I had a boss in Paris once that was a terror. I almost strangled him one day."

"Why didn't you?" the servant asked.

Muggs dropped the flaming match—into the filled wastebasket.

"Oh, somethin' happened to stop me—somebody got his lamps on me, or somethin'. And I didn't happen to get a chance again. I had to do a dodge. The cops was after me."

"Cops?"

"Say, I've had real cops after me in my day!" Muggs boasted. "I cut out that line of life a few years ago, when I met Mr. Verbeck, but before that I was somethin' of a terror—especially in Paris."

"Paris? I've never had a chance to go there," said the servant.

"You want to go when you get a roll, some time. It's some town, boy—*some* town!"

Muggs puffed at the cigarette again, and then turned toward the couch. The servant gave a cry and sprang from his chair.

"You cursed fool!" he shrieked. "You dropped that match in them papers!"

Muggs whirled around, astonishment in his face. "Put it out—or the whole darned place will burn down!" he cried. "If it catches on them curtains and things—"

He darted forward himself, snatched a small rug from the floor, and began beating at the flaming wastebasket. The servant was working on the other side of the table, trying to watch Muggs at the same time, but the latter seemed to be eager to put put the fire.

Muggs smashed at the flaming paper with his rug—and managed to scatter it. He ran from burning sheet to burning sheet, beating at the flames. The servant was not so watchful now. Muggs seemed intent only on putting out the fire and preventing a serious blaze; but as he fought the flames he managed now and then to thrust his hands and wrists into the fire!

The flames seared his flesh, but Muggs ignored that. He saw the cords that bound his wrists begin to smoke. He saw fire attack one of them. He thrust his wrists into the fire again, as he beat at a sheet of flaming paper, and tugged at his bonds. The fire was almost out now. He tugged at his bonds again.

They gave—they snapped—Muggs was free!

He gave a cry of relief, whirled around—launched himself straight at the Black Star's servant!

CHAPTER XXVIII

THE ALARM

The man realized in that instant that he had been tricked. He snarled like a beast and sprang to one side.

Muggs was upon him before he could utter a cry. They clashed, each trying to find the other's throat. Muggs found that this would be no easy battle. Here was a man who was used to rough tactics, such as did not meet with the approval of the Black Star.

Across the room they fought, Muggs trying to get the advantage, trying to keep the other from shrieking for help, trying to get in a blow that would silence his adversary for a time.

The servant fought to carry out his orders that Muggs should be kept prisoner; but Muggs fought with the knowledge that he was trying to prevent the Black Star from having success in his latest undertaking, trying to help Roger Verbeck to victory.

Back and forth across the room they continued to battle. They fought fiercely, and both were becoming exhausted. Now they were on their feet, wrestling, and now they were upon the floor, rolling over and over, striking at each other, reaching for each other's throat and eyes.

And finally Muggs managed to get the grasp for which he had been striving. The servant gave a groan of pain, and his hold on the valet relaxed. Muggs choked—choked, and finally sprang to his feet and looked down at the unconscious man.

He would be unconscious for some time, Muggs knew, as he did not intend to waste precious time binding and gagging him. He ran to the door through which the Black Star had gone, and stood there for a moment to listen. He heard nobody outside— remembered that nobody had been attracted by the sounds of combat.

Muggs lifted the curtain, opened the door, and stepped into a dark hall. He had no weapon, no electric torch, not so much as a match in his pocket. He ran lightly to the end of the hall and found another door. This he opened cautiously, an inch at a time. He found that it opened into a room that was dimly lighted, a room that did not seem to have seen much use.

Muggs hurried in and closed and locked the door behind him. On the opposite side there was another door; Muggs listened at that for a time, and then opened it. He found himself facing another hall.

He hurried into it, and went on. He came to a flight of stairs and went up. He realized, now, that he had been in a basement. At the top of the stairs was a large room, half filled with rusted machinery and empty packing cases.

Muggs stooped and picked up from the floor a short iron bar; he had a weapon now. On he went, across the big room to a window. He looked out.

He was in the manufacturing district, he knew. This building was an old, abandoned factory. He could see the yard filled with scrap iron, the high fence around it, and, beyond, the empty street. Farther beyond that was the city, flashing with light.

Muggs started to raise the window. It stuck, but he managed to pry it up with the bar of iron, stopping now and then to listen and watch. He couldn't convince himself that the Black Star had left no guard other than the servant now unconscious below. That wasn't at all like the Black Star, Muggs thought. There must be a trap somewhere.

Then he remembered that the Black Star had been forced to move quickly. Perhaps this headquarters had not been completed when the master criminal had taken up his abode there.

Muggs got the window up, put out his head and looked around. It was pitch dark beneath the window and along the wall. Muggs got through, lowered himself and dropped.

He crouched against the wall, listening, the bar of iron clutched in his hand, ready for instant fight if occasion demanded it. Then he started following the wall, going toward where he had noticed a gate in the high fence.

He reached the corner of the building, and glanced around it cautiously. Not far from him, he seemed to see something move. Muggs was not sure at first whether it was an elusive shadow or a man. He decided an instant later that it was a man.

He scarcely breathed now. He had escaped thus far, and he did not intend to be stopped. He did not intend to waste much time, either. Even now, perhaps, the Black Star and his followers were surrounding the Branniton residence. Even now, perhaps, they were robbing women of their jewels, rendering the three men they had decided to abduct unconscious, and preparing to carry them away.

Like a shadow, the iron bar held ready, Muggs crept along the wall in the direction of the guard.

He was within ten feet of him when a match glowed. The flame shot up, and Muggs could see that the match was burning in the man's cupped hands, and that he was trying to light a cigar. Muggs covered the ten feet in two springs, the iron bar swept through the air and landed. There was a little whimper, and the Black Star's guard was stretched on the ground.

Muggs turned and ran across the yard. He had decided not to try the gate, for there might be another guard there. He sprang, grasped the top of the fence, running the risk that it might be charged and deadly, found that such was not the case, and drew himself up. A moment later, he was in the street.

Muggs never had been much of a runner, but he ran tonight. Up the street he went, his elbows glued to his sides, head bent forward, stumbling and staggering over the rough cobblestones, but making excellent progress. There was no person on the street, no vehicle in sight. This was an old manufacturing district far down the river, where there was nothing to attract people. Only a few street lights were burning, and they were far apart.

Almost breathless, Muggs ran on. His heart was pounding at his ribs, his side pained, his breathing was labored. He turned a corner into another street, and continued running!

Would he never reach a telephone? Would he never run across a member of the police force? Was there nobody in that end of town who could help him? Block after block he ran, always looking for a light, for a dingy saloon, for some place where he could get into communication with police headquarters and give the alarm. He was in despair; he felt that he could not keep up much longer.

Presently he saw lights ahead of him, and felt hope and joy surge within him. Ahead, only two blocks away, was one of the barns of the city street railway.

Panting, exhausted, Muggs stumbled through the entrance and ran into the little office. Half a dozen conductors and motormen sprang from their benches and hurried toward him.

"Quick—telephone!" Muggs gasped. "Police—"

He saw the telephone instrument on the wall, and lurched toward it. He grasped the receiver, tore it from the hook, began calling into the transmitter. One of the conductors was trying to talk to him; one of the motormen was trying to stop him from using the instrument until he explained. Muggs threw out a foot and kicked him away.

"Police headquarters! Police headquarters!" he shrieked. "This headquarters? Give me the chief! This is Muggs! Yes—Muggs! Hurry—hurry!—That you, chief? Mr. Verbeck there? This is Muggs. I just—got away. Black Star's gang—going to raid—Branniton house—get jewels—kidnap them swells—"

And then Muggs sank slowly against the wall.

His words had electrified the conductors and motormen. They picked him up, and one of them continued the conversation, telling what had happened, but he soon found himself talking to nobody. The chief had recognized Muggs' voice and that had been enough.

The conductors and motormen threw water into Muggs' face, and he gasped and sat up. They helped him to a bench and sat him there, while he fought for breath, grasped his chest where it pained, struggled to regain his strength.

"Got—to get there—" he gasped.

"Where?" one of the men cried.

"Richard Branniton's house—in the—West End!"

"The foreman's flivver's out in front; he'll let us use it," a conductor cried. "I don't go on duty for an hour yet. Come on!"

He ran toward the curb, and Muggs staggered after him. Muggs got into the cheap little car. The obliging conductor cranked it and sprang in beside him.

"We'll get there quick, or we'll shake every bolt and nut off the blamed thing!" he said.

The flivver lurched away down the street.

* * * *

It would have done Muggs good had he been able to see the effect of his message at police headquarters. The chief sprang from his chair shrieking the news. Verbeck and the sheriff dashed with him through the assembly room and out to the street, and as they went, the chief shouted his orders. The reserves ran out and sprang into the automobiles, the deputies did the same.

"Good Muggs!" Verbeck cried, as he drove like a fiend through the streets. "I knew he'd do it—if he had a chance!"

Verbeck swung between two street cars, causing two motormen to turn pale for an instant, and then to curse joy riders. Strung out behind the powerful roadsters were the police cars. The sirens were not working now. The chief had issued orders that they were not to be used if it could be avoided, as it would indicate to the Black Star and his men that they were coming.

"Hope we get him this time!" the chief shrieked into Verbeck's ear. "Drive, man, drive!"

Verbeck drove. He forced the powerful roadster to do its utmost. He called upon the expensive engine to pay for itself this night. He swung around other vehicles, dashed around corners, swept up hills like a comet.

They passed through the retail district, and got on a wide avenue where there was not so much traffic, and where better speed could be made. And now they were in the section of better residences, speeding on.

They turned another corner—and the Branniton house was but four blocks away.

CHAPTER XXIX

CAUGHT IN THE NET

At the Branniton residence, Richard Branniton was stretched on the floor, unconscious from the effects of a vapor gun. The men were standing against one wall, the ladies against another. The Black Star's men guarded the doors and windows and watched the guests. The master criminal himself was in the center of the room.

"I must have all your jewels, ladies," he said. "You need not be alarmed; you shall not be harmed if you conduct yourselves properly. And you gentlemen will be safer if you indulge in no attempt to better your present condition. I assure you that you are at the mercy of my band."

He made a sign, and three of his men took bags from beneath their robes and started toward the line of women.

"Take off your jewelry and toss it into the bags," the Black Star directed. "Married ladies may retain their wedding rings and their engagement rings, but must give up everything else. That is just to show that I am not hard-hearted, as some persons would have the world believe."

He laughed gleefully as his men began their task. Terrified women removed their jewels and handed them over. Weeping women, hysterical women, surrendered necklaces, brooches, rings. The bags were filled rapidly, and the Black Star's men stepped back again.

"And now we have something else to do," the Black Star said. "Which of you gentlemen is Lord Sambery?"

One of them stepped forward, a dignified man of perhaps fifty. "I have that honor," he said stiffly.

"I admire you greatly, sir," the Black Star said. "I have read a great deal about the work you have done. I admire you so much that I insist you become my guest for a time."

"I beg your pardon?" stammered the astonished nobleman.

"I insist upon it, sir!" the Black Star said. "And where is Sir Burton Banks?"

"I am here!"

"I admire you, too, sir, and you shall be my guest also," the Black Star declared.

"Allow me to decline your hospitality," said Sir Burton Banks stiffly.

"But I cannot allow you to do so," the master criminal said, chuckling. "You see, you mean money to me."

"How is that?" Sir Burton Banks demanded.

"Not your money," the Black Star said. "It has occurred to us that you two gentlemen are in this country on an important mission, and that your time is very valuable. We have an idea that, if you should be detained, certain persons and personages would pay a handsome sum for your release."

"Why, confound the fellow! He means to abduct us and hold us for ransom!" Lord Sambery exclaimed.

"You have guessed it," the Black Star said.

"But this is the United States of America, sir, and we are in one of its greatest cities! I never heard of such a thing! The idea is preposterous! You can't do it!"

"Can't we?" asked the Black Star with a laugh. "It's a very simple thing. We just render you unconscious and carry you away—and you can never be found."

"Why, you dare not!" cried Sir Burton Banks.

"I am not particularly prone to fear," the master criminal said. "I have dared many things, and accomplished many things harder than kidnaping a couple of gentlemen. You need fear nothing; you shall be treated with every courtesy."

"I—I shall fight!" Lord Sambery declared.

"You are an elderly man, sir, and, also, I abhor violence," the

Black Star reminded him. "You cannot fight long against one of my vapor guns, your lordship."

"I—I—my country will have you punished for this!"

"The first thing will be to capture me, your lordship," said the master criminal. "I was captured before, but managed to escape, as perhaps you know. But we are wasting valuable time in conversation, and I'll have ample time to talk to you during the next two days. I am forced to have you gentlemen put to sleep for a short time, but I assure you there are no bad after effects."

"You—you—" Sir Burton stammered.

"It is quite useless to protest, or to attempt to fight," the Black Star informed him. "By the way, I am going to take Mr. Branniton along, too."

"You fiend!" Branniton's wife cried.

"He shall not be harmed, my dear madam, but it will cost him something to regain his liberty. He caused me considerable annoyance; he was the prosecuting attorney at my trial."

"And he shall be again!" Mrs. Branniton retorted.

"Perhaps—we shall see! I have no idea of standing trial again, my dear madam. By the time I am captured, your husband probably will be a United States senator, or an ambassador abroad. I realize that he is a man of promise."

The Black Star signaled to two of his men, and they advanced toward Lord Sambery and Sir Burton Banks. The latter showed that he intended to fight, regardless of what the master criminal had said. But the Black Star's men rushed in, discharged their vapor guns, and darted back again. The two diplomats toppled over on the floor. A woman shrieked.

"They are not harmed a bit," the Black Star assured them. "They will simply awake from a sleep, and feel quite fit. Ladies, I regret that I interrupted your little party. I suggest you continue it after I leave with my men. In reality, you should thank me. You will have something to talk about for the remainder of your lives; and women, I have heard, love to talk!"

He backed toward the entrance to the hall.

A shrill whistle came from the lawn outside—another—a third. The Black Star whirled toward the door. His men stood still, listening. Into the room rushed a robed and masked member of the band.

"Police, sir—all around the place!" he cried.

CHAPTER XXX

MUGGS ARRIVES

Verbeck's roadster was stopped on the corner nearest the Branniton residence. Verbeck and the chief sprang out and darted across the walk. The police autos came up and discharged their loads of officers. The chief issued his orders rapidly.

"Surround the place! Get into the alley! Pick up everybody that looks suspicious—and be ready to fight and fight hard! Let's get them this time!"

Officers hurried to every side of the house, poured into the alley, rushed across the lawn. They caught the men with the limousine, and those with the truck that apparently was stalled, and held them for investigation later. They drew a close net around the Branniton place, and the chief and Verbeck, with half a dozen trusted men, started toward the front veranda.

But the master criminal had had watchers scattered around the lawn. They were caught in the police net, too, but they were able to give the alarm. They rushed inside the house; and the Black Star was informed that the police were upon him.

He ordered the guests into one of the smaller rooms, and closed and locked the door on them. He had the lights turned off all over the house; the waiter attended to that. He issued his orders rapidly, like a general conducting a battle, sent men to defend the doors and windows.

"Violence appears to be necessary," he said. "We must drive them off and get away, or there'll be more of them upon us within a short time!"

From a window over the veranda, the Black Star looked at the situation. Two of the police automobiles were playing search-lights on the sides of the house. Another was driving across the lawn to do the same on the front. The Black Star took an automatic from beneath his robe, and fired one shot across the lawn.

The shot was a signal. From every window shots were sent at the men surrounding the house, shots that were not meant to wound or kill, only to terrify. But the chief's men were not easily frightened.

They sought refuge behind trees and clumps of brush, and returned the fire. They shattered windows and made it impossible for the Black Star's men to remain in them. They poured volleys against the doors.

But the master criminal and his men were safe so far. The officers were not able to get inside the house. The Black Star had no wish to stand a siege, for he knew that there could be but the one outcome. There came a lull in the battle, and the Black Star shouted from his window.

"Is the chief there?"

"He's here!" came a voice from the darkness.

"This is the Black Star!"

"Well, what do you want? Are you and your men ready to surrender to us? We'll get you, and get you good, if you don't!"

"Surrender?" the Black Star said. "When I hold the advantage?"

"I don't see it!" the chief shouted.

"No? My dear chief, there are in this house the most prominent persons in your fair city. We have with us, also, two diplomats of international fame. I abhor violence, but in such a case as this, it becomes necessary. You will withdraw your men. You will take them to the corner, beneath the electric light, where we can see them plainly. You will keep them there fifteen minutes, and after that you may do as you please."

"I see myself!" the chief cried.

"If you do not, I shall use violence upon those in the house. For every ten minutes we are forced to remain here, I shall take a human life. For every one of my men wounded or slain, I shall take another human life. Think it over, chief!"

The chief did think it over, with Roger Verbeck to aid him. The Black Star was at the end of his rope. Captured again, he was certain to be convicted and sentenced to prison for life. He was the sort who would go out fighting—the sort to do all the harm he could before he went out.

"We're not sure that it's not a bluff!" Verbeck said. "But we can't do as he asks, of course."

"We'll rush the house!" the sheriff declared. "That's our business in a case of this kind, isn't it? We may lose a few men, but it must be done. What else is there to do?"

"We'll have to rush it!" the chief returned. "Our aim is to get inside and fight it out as quickly as possible, without letting that fiend have time to do much damage. I'll give the orders." The chief whispered them to a captain, and he passed them on.

The Black Star was shouting from a window again. "'Well, what is the decision, chief?"

"You say you want fifteen minutes?" the chief asked, more to gain time than anything else.

"Fifteen minutes will be enough, thank you. Remain on that corner with your men for fifteen minutes, and then do as you please. That is all I ask."

"Well, you're asking enough! What do you suppose the public will say when they know I had you and let you go?"

"My dear chief, they'll probably give you credit for saving the lives of some prominent persons. I understand that the mayor is a guest here this evening. Shall I have him come to the window and decide what you are to do?"

"Let him come!" the chief said.

He knew in advance what the mayor would say. The mayor would tell him to charge the house, break in, and capture the Black Star and his men. The mayor happened to be a man of courage.

Thus the chief had gained a little time, and that was all he wanted—time enough for his orders to be passed around to all the officers. Now his men were ready.

The chief blew his whistle. The searchlights that had been playing on the house were extinguished; and through the darkness the police and deputies rushed upon the Branniton residence!

A volley greeted them from the windows, but the Black Star's men were firing wildly into the darkness, and their shots had no effect. Officers and deputies crowded the veranda, attacked the French windows, battered at the doors.

A cheap automobile lurched around the corner and stopped in front of the house. Muggs had arrived!

CHAPTER XXXI

AN EMPTY NET

Muggs never forgot that wild ride in the flivver. The street-car conductor drove the little machine as if it had been a racing car. It lurched around corners, almost ran down traffic policemen, swung ahead of street cars. The conductor was like a maniac. He always had craved excitement and adventure. Now it had come to him, and he intended to make the most of it.

They dashed up to the Branniton residence, and Muggs, not even thinking of thanking the conductor, sprang out and rushed across the lawn.

"Boss! boss!" he shrieked above the din.

Somebody told him that Verbeck was on the veranda. He rushed there and found his employer.

"Boss, was I in time?" he asked. "I got loose as soon as I could!"

"You bet you were, Muggs. The Black Star's inside, with some of his gang!"

"I told the big stiff this was goin' to be his unlucky night! You give me a chance to get at him, boss! I've got a few scores to settle with that bird!"

"We'll all get at him, Muggs! We'll be inside in a minute!"

The doors and windows were crashing in now. Policemen and deputies were pouring into the house. Shots greeted them, shots from both automatics and vapor guns. They struggled through clouds of the pungent vapor, here and there a man dropping because he had inhaled some of the fumes. They grappled with men in black robes and masks. Through the house they fought, while outside were others who watched every exit and caught those who tried to get away from the place.

One of the deputies had been an electrician formerly, and he knew where the light switches were located in the Branniton house. He fought his way to the kitchen, found them, and turned on the lights.

Things were better for the policemen and deputies after that. They could tell friends from foes. The Black Star's men barricaded themselves in certain rooms. Some of them threw down their weapons and held up their hands in token of surrender, and were immediately seized and handcuffed. The others were cleared from the lower floor, fought up the wide stairs, and continued the battle on the second floor.

Verbeck and Muggs were in the thick of the fight. They were looking for the Black Star. So were the chief, and Sheriff Kowen. They searched the basement and the rooms on the ground floor, but found no trace of him.

"He's on the second floor!" Verbeck cried. "Up we go!"

The guests who had been held prisoners were released from the room in which they had been locked. The women fled to the lawn, and across it to the street. Some of the men went with them; others joined in the fray. There was a crowd in the street now and more people were arriving every minute. Word had flashed throughout the city that the Black Star and his followers had been cornered in the residence of Richard Branniton.

The members of the band were being caught rapidly. A few had been wounded, a few officers also. But the criminals were scattered now, and here and there one surrendered, or was overpowered.

Verbeck and Muggs, the chief and the sheriff thought of nothing but the Black Star. They knew that the policemen and deputies could care for the others of the band. It was the master criminal himself that they wanted, to put him behind prison bars once more, to have years added to his sentence, to send him to the big prison up the river where he no longer would be a menace to society at large.

They ran from room to room, searching for him. They shrieked suggestions to one another above the din of the battle. They found a room at one end of the upper hall, with the door locked, and hurled themselves against it and broke it in.

There they saw the man they wanted. He had thrown off his robe and mask. He held a bomb in his hand—and stopped them with a gesture.

"Wait!" he commanded. "This is not a vapor bomb—it is the real thing. It can blow all of us to bits! So four of you came to get me, eh? Mr. Verbeck, and the chief and the sheriff—and Muggs. I suppose, since you are free and here, that you did all this, Muggs?"

"You bet I did!" Muggs cried.

"Wait, gentlemen! Don't make a move to raise a weapon, or we all will be hurled into the hereafter." The Black Star stepped back toward a window. "I suppose you have me cornered," he said. "I suppose you think you are going to take me back to jail. But it happens that I have one card yet to play!"

He hurled the bomb, and it exploded. It was a vapor bomb, after all. The cloud of pungent gas assailed them. They whirled to either side, away from it. There was a crash of glass.

"He's gone through the window!" Muggs shrieked.

Trying to keep from breathing, they rushed to the window, got through it and to the roof of the veranda, where they gulped the fresh air!

The Black Star had jumped to the ground. They saw him for an instant. Then he was lost in the darkness. The chief shouted a warning to his men.

"Down, and after him!" Verbeck cried.

"We've got him!" cried the chief. "The entire yard is surrounded. He's in a trap!"

Muggs was the first to reach the ground. He did not stop to climb down one of the posts, but did as the master criminal had done—jumped.

Verbeck and the chief and Sheriff Kowen were not far behind him. Officers who had been on the veranda charged after the Black Star in response to the chief's command.

The net grew tighter. They were in a corner of the lawn, calling to one another. A police auto drove across the grass, and the searchlight was turned on.

There was the circle of policemen and deputies, with Verbeck and Muggs, the chief and the sheriff at one side of it.

But the Black Star was gone!

CHAPTER XXXII

THE LETTER

"He can't have got away!" Muggs exclaimed.

"Where did he go?" the chief demanded.

"He didn't come past us," one of the policemen declared. "I don't see how he got out of the circle. Why, he hasn't had time to get away; and the men in the street—"

The officers in the street already had been warned. The entire block was surrounded; it seemed impossible that the master criminal could escape.

"Maybe he dodged the boys here, but he'll never get away from the block!" the chief declared. "Have more searchlights turned on the lawn, and tell the men in the alley to keep awake. He can't be far!"

Out of the sky came a blinding light. It flooded the house and lawn, turned the night into day.

"That—that light—" Sheriff Kowen gasped.

The light disappeared. They waited, watching the sky. They were silent now. No sound reached their ears except the din from the house. They saw nothing.

And then they heard the Black Star's voice.

"Did you really think you had me?" it said. "I must admit that you have wrecked my plans and scattered my organization again. Some of my men will have to go to prison, I suppose, but you haven't caught me, never will catch me! I shall leave the city, and you cannot prevent it. I have prepared for this emergency. When my organization is formed again, perhaps I shall return. My campaign is over for the present, but there will be another!"

The voice died away. There was silence for a moment, and

then the brilliant light flashed again, flooded the lawn, almost blinded the men there.

"There is a letter by the alley gate!" The voice of the Black Star now came to them faintly. "Good night, gentlemen!"

"Gone!" the chief gasped. "Gone!"

"But how on earth—" Kowen began.

"That letter!" Verbeck cried. "Let's get it!" They hurried to the alley gate, and there they found the letter, as the Black Star had said. They carried it back to the police automobile, and read it in front of the searchlight.

Gentlemen: If you have this letter, it means that my plans have been ruined, and that I have been forced to escape. I cannot neglect this chance to tell you how futile have been your efforts.

Have you wondered how I spoke to you out of the sky? Have you worried about the bright light? Are you surprised at the way I escaped you just now?

I have in my organization a wonderful man. He is a mechanical genius gone wrong. He has perfected airplanes as no man dreams they can be perfected. I have been using an airplane—but it is a *noiseless* airplane! Can you imagine what that would mean if the world had the secret? An airplane, as the public knows it, heralds its approach. With this, I can sail at night over the city, without making the slightest noise. I can hover over a certain spot—

Yes, I mean *hover*. For this airplane is so perfected that it can stand still in the air. It can be raised or lowered straight up or down. Do you understand now?

The airplane was hovering over the lawn, a rope ladder dropped from it. I merely climbed up the ladder as the airplane ascended. I am writing this in advance, but I know what I shall do, if forced. I always plan for every emergency, you see. And while you poor fools bite your nails in your chagrin, I shall be speeding through the air to a certain refuge I have prepared. There I shall recuperate and plan some more.

Roger Verbeck read the letter aloud. A chorus of gasps came from those who heard.

"Well, he is gone!" Verbeck said. "But his band is broken up, and that is something!"

"And if he ever comes back here, we'll get him, won't we, boss?" Muggs asked.

"We'll get him!" Roger Verbeck said. There was determination in his voice.